Original Book Cover & Character Art by @GloInkDesigns, Athira Jayachandran.

Discreet Book Cover Art by @LemonLee.Shop, Megan Lee.

Comprehensive Editing @EJLEditing, EJ Lounsbury.

Proofreaders: @weloveamagicalread, Cassidy Galewski. @getawaypages, Chelsey Theriac.

1st edition 2025.

Coffee People

Brews, Blooms, and Books #1

Ashley Claire

For everyone who still doesn't know what they want to be when they grow up.
Life is about learning and growing. You're "enough" just the way you are.

What does a coffee lover say when
they're hitting on you?
I've bean thinking about you a latte.

Content Warning

Dear Family and Friends,

Thanks for buying my book.

This book however is a romance novel and has a certain amount of spice to it, smut if you will.

If you would like to continue to look at me as "that little girl I used to babysit" or "my sweet friend who is always kind," then I kindly ask you to put the book down now.

Seriously, thanks for buying my book, but if reading it will cause you to not be able to look at me the same way over the potatoes at Thanksgiving, then stop here.

This was your warning <3

Love you bunches, XOXO Ashley

Other Actual Content Warnings:

- Death of a Parent

- Grief

- Explicit Sexual Content

- Vulgar Language

- Alcohol use

- Depression

- Predatory Business

Coffee People Playlist

Espresso
Sabrina Carpenter

Risk
Gracie Abrams

Packing it up
Gracie Abrams

Get him back
Olivia Rodrigo

Bad Blood
Taylor Swift

Good Graces
Sabrina Carpenter

Sweet Nothing
Taylor Swift

Nobody but You
Blake Sheldon

There She Goes
Benson Boone

**Here with me
(Ft. CHVRCHES)**
Marshmello

You are in Love
Taylor Swift

A-O-K
Tai Verdes

There She Goes
Sixpence None the Richer

Sleep Deprivation
Chance Pena

Can't Stop
Red Hot Chili Peppers

Heart Shaped Box
Nirvana

Afternoon Delight
Starland Vocal Band

**Signed, Sealed, Delivered
I'm yours**
Stevie Wonder

Dreams
The Cranberries

Thinking Out Loud
Ed Sheeran

CHAPTER ONE

Sarah

It's been three days since I've seen the love of my life.

Okay, maybe he's not *really* the love of my life, but the man is an absolute dream.

He comes into my coffee shop every morning and orders the perfect drink. He gives me the perfect smile. He even leaves a cash tip! He is my dream man, and yes, I am basing that off his coffee order alone.

When you've been working in the coffee industry for twelve years, you can tell a lot about a person based on their coffee order. I've got it down to a science. I can take one glance at a person as they walk into my shop and know exactly what they will order. Am I occasionally wrong? Yes. About once or twice a year, I'm completely off. The majority of the time, however, I can definitely judge people by their order.

That's the thing about paying attention, staying quiet, and reading people. If you stop and listen, just observe, you can learn a lot about the people around you. I can do all of those things while people order their coffee.

My order, well, I don't order my coffee; I make it. In the town of Daisy Ridge, I *am* coffee. I started working in a coffee shop in the next town over when I was sixteen. I worked there on the weekends through high school and then continued working there after I graduated. Even though my plan was to leave this small town after getting my degree online, I couldn't bring myself to leave.

Daisy Ridge is something of a conundrum to most people. With a population of only 7,000 people, we aren't your typical small town. We are more of a pit stop, nestled right off a highway. We are the last stop before the gas prices start to creep up on your way into the big city. We have one grocery store and two fast-food joints—McDonald's and Burger King. I opened my coffee shop as close to the highway exit as I could get. My hope was that travelers would stop here for one last hit of caffeine on their way to somewhere new and exciting.

On most days, traffic through Daisy Ridge is great. Other times, though, it seems like it's just me and the other 6,999 people who live here.

My Daisy Ridge Coffee Co. sign can be seen from the highway, and I must say it is awfully cute and draws in a lot of the female population passing through. I took the name literally and had daisy flowers added to both sides of the sign a few years back. The front porch is small but enough for three small round tables and six chairs.

My coffee shop is my favorite place in the world, a little two-story shop on the main street of Daisy Ridge. It's comfortable and homey. I live right above the coffee shop, but it doesn't connect and has its own entrance in the back, which everyone always says is a good thing because if it didn't, I'd probably never leave the shop.

If someone saw me walking into their coffee shop, they would probably guess that I would order a flavored iced latte. Which happens to be correct. Most people think that in order to own a coffee business, you need to drink black coffee or dark plain espresso out of tiny cups, but that's not me. You *do* need to know the science behind the roast and the flavor palettes of the beans. However, I love making all kinds of fun-flavored drinks. That's where my passion is. I love seeing what flavors will pair well together or trying to replicate the flavor of a specific cookie or muffin I enjoy in my free time.

Anyway, back to the man who has stolen my heart. His name is Liam, and he moved to Daisy Ridge about six months ago. Why? I haven't found out yet. I'm still working up the courage to say anything more than the exchange of his coffee order and our basic pleasantries.

Liam always says hi, smiles, and says please and thank you. He seems like a genuinely nice human, *and* he orders Sarah's Special. Which is a drink of my own creation: a perfect latte I made to taste just like my favorite Girl Scout cookie, a Samoa. It's delicious and certainly not nutritious in any way. He loves it, though, and even better? He orders it iced, which is the way I prefer it.

While it's not *my* daily drink, Liam has ordered it every day. A fact that makes my coffee-judging heart flutter. I'm not sure if he even knows that I am Sarah or that he orders my special every day. Over the last six months, I've observed him enough, and he has captured my heart. Enough that I now casually call him the "love of my life" in my mind, even though I've never been in love.

I know that's insane for a twenty-eight-year-old woman to be calling a perfect stranger the "love of my life", but it's true. I just know it; consider it love at first sight.

The bell to my small coffee shop dings, and in walks my only employee who isn't related to me, Carol. She's a feisty fifty-four-year-old woman who has lived in Daisy Ridge her whole life. She's old enough to be my mom. In fact, she is older than my mom would be.

My mom died when I was a child. My dad is an awesome guy, so don't start feeling super bad. Yes, it sucks losing a parent. Even after all these years, there are some days where I wake up and feel like my body is made of lead and I cannot bring myself to get out of my bed. It helps though, to know she would be happy with who my sister, Jess, and I have become. She would not be disappointed when looking at the little life my dad helped us make here in Daisy Ridge. Especially since she loved Daisy Ridge almost as much as she loved us.

However, she might be truly disappointed that I don't date. She was a hopeless romantic in every way. She loved fairytales and romantic comedies. She would dance around the kitchen with my dad every Sunday morning while he made us pancakes.

So needless to say, she would be disappointed that I don't date, but I just enjoy working *way* too much. I always have. When I go home after work, I like to snuggle on the couch with my cat, Trixie, read a great book, and down a glass of chardonnay.

I shake my head and glance over at Carol, who has made her way behind the counter now. She looks feisty as ever today, wearing all leopard print and her hot pink cowboy boot earrings. Her wild strawberry blonde curls are spilling out of a sparkly silver hair tie. Carol goes to our one and only local yoga class most mornings, and you would *never* guess she is fifty-four, but she will tell *everyone* exactly how old she really is. She has zero filter and holds nothing back. She's spunky and supportive and has been nothing but an amazing employee and friend over the years. She is just so perfectly *Carol*.

Carol throws on her hot pink Daisy Ridge Coffee Co. apron that she made herself with embroidered daisies on it. Then she walks up and grabs my hand, which is unusual by the way, and says in her thick Southern drawl, "Hun, I've got some real bad news."

My mind immediately goes to Liam, who hasn't come in the past three days. Did she hear what happened to him? Did he move away? Get in a car accident? My mind starts racing a mile a minute.

Carol snaps her fingers in front of my face. She can obviously tell I've been in a trance for the past twenty minutes. It's been a *really* slow morning here. It definitely feels like no one is passing through town today. There is a slow drizzle outside, so maybe it'll pick up if and when the sun decides to show up later.

"Hun, I *said* I have some bad news. I just came from the town meeting."

Ahhhh yes, the good ol' town meeting. Have you ever seen the show *Gilmore Girls*? You know how basically every meeting has this crotchety older man yelling at everyone about how they can't do things? But simultaneously wants them to volunteer for a million things? Then there are a bunch of spunky old townsfolk demanding weird things? Yeah, it's *exactly* like that.

I sigh. "What's dear ole Mayor Leopold up to now?" I ask her.

"He's letting them put in a . . . you-know-what."

Oh nooooo! Oh no! They *cannot* put in a Starbucks here. I'll be screwed. Sure, all the town locals will still come here, but the travelers? The people passing through? They'll go to the chain they know and love. Oh god. *Oh god*. My chest starts to tighten. Am I breathing?

"HE'S WHAT?" I shout.

The door chimes again, and in walks Liam, the love of my life . . . dear gosh, what terrific timing for the man of my dreams. *Ugh*, I start to roll my eyes and then realize he *definitely* just heard me shouting at Carol.

Cool, cool, cool. All is good. Deep breaths, Sarah.

I look over at Liam.

"Hey, you! Haven't seen you in a while. Large iced Sarah's Special?"

Pulling out his wallet, he smiles that same perfect smile and says, with a wink, "Yes! That would be great!"

I give him my best smile back and let him know, "It'll be out in a jiff!" and I immediately want to smack myself in the face. Did I just use the word *jiff*? Oh good lord, it's going to be a really long day.

I'm starting up the espresso machine and tamping my espresso behind the counter, so I nod over at Carol. "Mind ringing him up for me?"

She smiles. "Not at all, Boss Lady."

She loves calling me boss to stir up trouble. It always gets folks riled up and asking questions about how a fifty-four-year-old woman ended up working for some sassy twenty-eight-year-old. Liam, of course, doesn't take the bait, though. He actually just glances down at his phone.

It's odd. He usually doesn't use his phone here.

Carol rings him up, and I finish making Liam's coffee and hand it over to him.

Liam looks up from his phone, glances at his drink, and then looks up into my eyes. "Actually, do you mind adding some caramel drizzle today? You did it a couple of weeks ago, and it was magical." He winks at me. My heart could practically melt into a puddle on the floor.

He *winked*.

"Of course, anything for you, Liam!" I smile while adding caramel drizzle to the top of his drink. It feels almost seductive, the way we stare into each other's eyes while I drizzle the syrup.

I finish and put the lid back on, handing him his extra caramelly drink.

Liam, who is still passionately staring into my eyes, says, "Thanks, Sarah! Mind if I use your Wi-Fi for a while today? I was hoping to sit and get some work done in here."

I inform him that the Wi-Fi password is on the far left bookshelf. He says a quick "Thanks!" and heads to find a seat. Obviously, I couldn't be happier to hear that Liam plans to sit and work in my coffee shop, *and* he used my name. Hearing my name come out of his mouth does something absolutely foreign to my stomach. It's been a looong time since I've been interested in a man—small-town problems.

If it weren't for our small town, I probably wouldn't get a second glance from most men. Or women, for that matter. The lack of other females in this town has helped me out over the years. I'm 5'2" on a good day, and while my family genetics mean I'm naturally leaner, I'm certainly not fit. I live in black leggings that are typically covered in cat hair. My thick dark brown hair doesn't hold a curl anymore, and with running the shop, leaving it down is out of the question. Most days, I toss it up in a bun or a large claw clip.

I look around the shop because now I'm paranoid. He hasn't ever sat down and worked in here before. The floors are clean, and fresh flowers decorate every table. My little sister, Jess, loves creating arrangements for my café and has dreams of heading to a big city someday to do florals for weddings. I truly hope she makes that dream a reality soon, but for now, she works part-time for me and takes a floral design class once a week. She also spends some of her free time making cute arrangements for my coffee shop, and I couldn't be more grateful.

I have to say I'm incredibly happy with her current arrangements. They aren't too feminine, mostly white lilies and greenery, and they match my light sage green

walls perfectly. Luckily, the bookshelves also look orga-
nized and tidy today.

Honestly, I first moved a single bookshelf into the shop
because I was running out of space in my upstairs apartment. When I brought some books down, the locals loved
it. It drew in people for longer periods of time, so as more
and more books came into the shop, I added more bookshelves. Now I've got three bookshelves full of different
genres lining the walls.

Of course, I keep my spicy romance books at home. I
don't need any of the locals borrowing those and wanting
to chat about them later.

I have another area with kid's games, LEGO sets, and
Lincoln Logs, which are always a hit with the travelers
heading off with their kiddos. It's a win-win because the
kids love stretching their legs and playing a game or two,
while the parents love to fuel up on coffee for the next two
hours of driving before hitting the city of Rose Point.

Overall, everything currently appears clean and orga-
nized, so I'm happy and calm when Liam finds his seat over
in the corner.

I peek back over at Carol, who is texting on her phone.
I walk over and whisper to her, "Are you sure they are
building their location *here*? In *Daisy Ridge*? I didn't think
they ever would at this point. I mean, why would they?"

Carol stops texting and looks up at me. "It was made
quite clear in the town meeting that the location is *here*."

I let out an exasperated sigh. My business is great, boom-
ing even. But this is going to be a problem.

CHAPTER TWO

Ethan

I HATE MY JOB.

Listen, I know how that sounds, but I do, and I know it pays super well. I know I should put up and shut up. I just *can't*.

I work in construction. It was actually my dad's business, and when he suddenly passed away last year, I had a responsibility to take over the business for a while. So say hello to the new owner and Area Manager of BloomStone Builders.

I'm not sure I've even properly grieved the loss of my dad, just the loss of a life I loved instead. Again, I know that sounds really shitty, but it's just the facts of my life right now.

Now that I'm here, though, I'm just not sure what else I could do with my life. I'm not book-smart, and I don't have the experience to do much. I worked for a coffee shop in a big city prior to taking over my dad's company.

I never wanted to work for my dad, even though he always offered. He knew I was happy just working at the coffee shop and biking around the city in my free time. I took over now because I have four younger brothers who *really* want this job. I just need to keep everything afloat until they finish their college degrees and can take over my position, so I'm a placeholder for now. While that's not something I'm proud of, it's temporary.

Luckily, keeping BloomStone Builders a success has been pretty easy so far. I got a major deal with Starbucks, freaking *Starbucks*, for the company to design and construct several new locations in their United States Southwest Region.

The contract ends in two years after we build out six new locations. The money is fantastic; the employees are excited. It's been ideal for everyone involved—except me, who hates traveling around, designing, and construction.

Honestly, I'm just not cut out for this life. I'm a homebody who enjoys coffee and good movies. I'm an introverted guy who likes to hike alone in my free time. I also enjoy running and biking occasionally, but it's mostly just so I can continue to eat whatever I want and stay in shape.

My mom actually had me at sixteen, and my real dad left her as soon as the pee on the stick dried. I've never met him, even though I know exactly where he lives. I don't care to meet someone like that. If he didn't want me in his life, I don't need him.

My mom ended up with the man I've called Dad my entire life when I was five. He was perfect for her. They gave me an ideal example of a happy and healthy marriage.

He legally adopted me when they got married. He didn't have to love me as his own all those years ago, so the least I can do is try to carry on his legacy for his "real" sons—my younger brothers. There is an age gap between us, considering my mom was only sixteen when I was born. My oldest "little" brother, Eric, is twenty-two and hopefully graduating from college this year. Out of all my younger brothers, he and I are, without a doubt, the closest.

We talk the most frequently, and my other younger brothers and I just have a pretty big age gap. Don't get me wrong—I love them. We just never really did a lot together like Eric and I have.

I've got my fingers crossed that Eric graduates on time this year so I can hand this life over to him as quickly as possible.

I'm excited to pass this off to him because I'm struggling to manage everything right now. He will be *much* more qualified to do this job, not to mention he will have the proper degree to do it. The only reason things are going well for the company right now is because of our deal with Starbucks and the amazing employees of BloomStone Builders. They are way too kind to me and have helped me learn the ropes. They know I'm just a placeholder for a younger brother who will do the job justice, and they have not complained for a single second about some young kid with no construction experience showing up and taking over.

On the other hand, when this is all over, I'm unsure of what I'll do next, and honestly, it's embarrassing. It feels like I should have it figured out by now—I'm almost thirty for Christ's sake! All I know is that I want to be happy, but doing something that makes you happy doesn't always pay well. It's not exactly the kind of job that draws in the ladies.

I wish more people would tell you it's okay to be almost thirty and still not know what you want to be when you grow up. I wish it wasn't completely frowned upon to not have my shit together at this age.

But mostly, I wish people would understand that not everyone is going to have some high-paying, high-class job. Some of us *want* to work on the "little" things. Some of us were twenty-seven-year-olds who truly enjoyed being *just* a coffee shop employee. Some of us enjoy being an employee and don't have the high ambitions of being the boss.

I'm lost in all of my thoughts as I'm driving down the highway in my beat-up red two-door Jeep. I'm on my way to meet with my "friend" Liam. The guy is a real jerk, if I'm being honest, but he works pretty high up at Starbucks. He is the one who originally helped me score this killer deal, so I kind of owe him one right now. Luckily, shortly after the deal, he was assigned to go scout one of the new locations. He was tasked with figuring out what land was for sale, where a location would work best, what competition may be in the area, etc. He has been out in this area for about six months now, and it's been great for me.

Like I said, the guy is a jerk, but he was my dad's best friend's son, so I have to put up with him for the time being. He always tells everyone we are good friends, and he *has* helped me out a lot over the past year.

My phone starts ringing, and I answer it on speaker-phone in my car, which is too old to have a Bluetooth setting.

"Hi, Ethan Stone speaking."

"What up, my main man! You almost here?"

Ughhhhhh. It's Liam already. I'm going to need the strongest caffeine kick every day to survive dealing with this guy for this long.

"Oh. Hey, man. I'm actually still about thirty-five minutes out. Didn't realize how far into the middle of nowhere this was."

Liam sighs. "Oh yeah, man. It's been rough, but I finally found a few hot girls to keep me company. The one I've been seeing recently said she can set you up with her sister while you're here."

Perfect, just perfect. The last thing I want to do is meet someone in this secluded area where there is nothing to do.

"I think I'm okay, actually. I just need to get this job done, and I would feel bad leading someone on out here. I would *never* actually live here. . ."

"Dude, we aren't falling in love, just going on some dates. It'll be fun!" I can hear Liam typing, and then I hear an espresso machine in the background. "All right, man, it's getting a little loud in here. I'll see you when you get here. Don't forget, I'm at the Daisy Ridge Coffee Company." He hangs up.

How could I forget? I think it's rather shitty of him to set up a meeting *inside* the shop of what he says is the *only* competition. But at the same time, the coffee is probably so gross in some little Podunk coffee shop in the middle of nowhere. I think I'd rather meet at the McDonald's in town. Their coffee is probably better.

CHAPTER THREE

Sarah

I MAKE MY WAY to the back office and close the door. *Deep breaths, Sarah. It's all going to work out.* I'll repeat it to myself over and over until I'm blue in the face.

Today is just not my day. I take a big sip of a new iced latte I'm testing, chocolate-covered strawberry . . . . *YUM.* I set it down on my desk and open up my computer. I'm going to work on some spreadsheets, order more inventory, and focus on the present. I'll find a way to make this work. I've needed to revamp my business for a while now, so this will finally give me the perfect push I need to do it.

My cell phone rings. I reach over to grab it without looking and knock my iced latte everywhere. *Shit. Shiiiiiiiiiit. Where are the freaking paper towels?*

I answer the phone with an exasperated and loud "Hello?!"

"Woah, is that how we greet each other these days? I thought I was your favorite sister?"

Of course it's my little sister who is calling right now, and even though she's twenty-five years old, I'm *sure* it's because she needs something.

"Hi, Jess. First of all, you're my only sister. Second, I just spilled my latte, yelled in front of my dream man, *and* found out they are opening a Starbucks in town." I let out a sigh and start trying to clean up the mess with a stack of Burger King napkins I find in my drawer. "I'm just . . . having a really rough day . . . What's up?"

Jess lets out a squeal of delight. "Then I have the *perfect* thing to cheer you up!" She takes a deep breath, and I know deep in my bones this will not be perfect, it most definitely will *not* cheer me up, and it is probably more for her than me. Jess squeals again before saying, "How about a date with a super-hot guy?"

Wow, that is . . . not what I expected at all. "Uhm, I'm not really in the mood, Jess."

"Sarah, *pleeeeease.* I never ask you for anything at all! Like, ever!" Uhm, except she does ask me for things . . . all the time? "I want to go on a date with a guy I met at the grocery store last week. But he has a friend in town—a friend who is around your age and crazy hot. I can't go on my date unless we find someone to entertain his sexy friend. He doesn't want to leave his friend hanging. Isn't that so sweeeet?"

No, I don't think it is cute. I think that's super freaking weird, because what grown man can't be alone for a night while his friend goes on a date? He should be able to leave this man-child alone for one stinking dinner.

Jess takes a huge mighty breath. "*Please,* Sarah, please, please, *pleaaaaase.* I really need this. This guy is just so . . . perfect for me."

I sigh. I mean, I get it, and I get where she gets this from. She's a hopeless romantic just like Mom was. She sees the beauty in everything. I just honestly have no interest in doing this, though. "Jess, let me think about this. I have a lot going on right now, and you know I need time to relax."

Jess grunts, and I can almost feel her anger seeping through the phone. "Sarah, your idea of relaxing consists of romance novels and wine. Trixie won't get lonely, I promise. She'll be perfectly fine, in fact. So why not go *live* in one of the romance novels you love so much?"

Now she is making me mad, too. "Jess, romance novels are *fiction.* Reality is gross and not romantic at all. That's why I don't bother. Do you even know this guy?"

"No, Sarah. That's why I need to go on a *date.* To see if we are compatible. Just please come with me. I'll pick you up at eight!"

Jess hangs up the phone before I can even respond.

She's a stupid brat because she knows I was about to argue that eight p.m. is way too late for me. I fully planned on being in my pajamas and reading my new Emily Henry novel at that time.

UGHHH, I'm completely over today. I need to wash my hands of this day, go to sleep, and hope for a better one tomorrow.

I continue cleaning up the mess from the iced latte I spilled, and when I've finally finished, there is a knock on my office door.

"Come in!" I shout. Carol pokes her head in.

"Hey, boss! I can't find any hot coffee sleeves."

Crap. "Okay, I'll be right there!" I close my laptop and head back into the store.

I head over to the cabinet where we store the extra cups when Liam yells, "Hey!"

My palms start sweating, and my heart starts racing. "He—" I turn around, only to realize he isn't talking to me. He's talking to some man in a suit, with an annoyed expression on his face, who just walked into the store.

I close my mouth before he realizes I embarrassingly thought he was talking to me.

The man who walked in the front door is hot, don't get me wrong. However, I know he is about to order a large hot Americano. Ick, he is definitely not my type. He's of course tall—maybe just over six feet—with dark brown hair and incredibly handsome. He is really muscular, like he could be a professional athlete or something? I suppose he very well might be with the expensive-as-heck suit he is wearing. *What the hell? Is he wearing a Rolex? Do people even wear those anymore?*

I just know he can't possibly be a professional athlete, though. Most athletes are dopey and smile a lot. They order things like frappes or a fancy cold brew. This guy in front of me looks as if he hasn't cracked a smile in a decade. Which is exactly why he is about to order a large hot Americano. People who order hot Americanos when it's warm here in the Southwest don't smile much.

I'm rummaging through the cabinet again, because I can tell this guy is going to be the type of man to get mad if I don't have a silly stinking coffee sleeve for his stupid hot coffee.

"Large hot Americano," the brooding, grumpy man says to Carol at the register as I smile into the cabinet. I've still got it. I *know* what people will order.

CHAPTER FOUR

Ethan

I TAKE A LOOK around at the coffee shop Liam asked me to meet him in. It isn't at all what I expected. I honestly probably could have ordered something different. Based on the coffee shop, the beans I can see behind the counter, and the brand of syrups they use, this will likely be a decent cup of coffee. However, I had already ordered before I noticed any of these things.

Plus, I'm going to need a million shots of espresso to make it through even just a few hours with Liam. I'm incredibly uncomfortable in my dad's old suit and watch.

Unfortunately, I didn't exactly have a closet full of professional clothes ready to go when I took over this job so suddenly. The watch is actually really nice, though. Every time I look at the time, I feel a little bit like my dad is still here. I miss him a lot. I feel like it's been a long time since I've laughed or smiled. I've been deep under a mountain of my grief.

This coffee shop reminds me of the one I loved working in. It doesn't appear to be a chain, but I think they should have a couple more locations.

They have a kids' area, books, fresh flowers, and a spot for dogs outside—all incredibly thoughtful touches that make people feel comfortable instantly.

I'm curious about the exterior of this shop, though, as it's a two-story building. I wonder if the upstairs is also part of the café.

I glance at the two women behind the counter. I'll admit that I was too distracted by Liam and completely tired and grumpy from my long drive, that I truthfully didn't even look up at them until now. Which I immediately regret, as I remember my time as a barista.

Good lord, one of them is incredibly quirky with her thick red curls an absolute mess. She looks like your typical 'small-town citizen.' As she turns, I notice she is wearing a name tag on her apron that says *Carol*. Her leopard print clothes are almost as wild as her hair. I immediately like her, and just like other parts of the café, she instantly makes you feel at ease.

The other one . . . is gorgeous. She is a mess, don't get me wrong, but I don't think I've ever seen a more beautiful woman. She looks like she was made for me. With hair piled on top of her head and rosy cheeks, she is rummaging around through a cupboard while huffing. She has beautiful curves that are accentuated by her tight black leggings, and she's wearing a Grateful Dead T-shirt that is too big for her. Her Converse are faded and look well-loved. I look at them with envy, wishing I was wearing my own Converse right now and not these stupid dress shoes.

I glance away quickly so she doesn't see me staring. I glance back over at Carol on the register. She is smirking at me and shoots me a wink as my stomach does a pancake flip. I hope she doesn't tell her coworker that she saw my little ogling episode. She turns around to start up the espresso machine.

The beautiful woman finds whatever it was she was searching for and tells Carol she is heading to the back. She doesn't even glance my way.

Chapter Five

Sarah

I FOUND THE COFFEE sleeves quickly enough that Mr. Americano didn't have to throw a fit about his stupid hot coffee burning his big dumb hand.

I start to head for the back, but I linger in the hallway for a moment. I peek around the corner to sneak another glance at Liam. Mr. Americano sits down with Liam at his table, and he's already scowling about something.

His chiseled jaw is tense as he begins a deep conversation with Liam. I'm sure it's because Mr. Americano hates my fresh flowers and bookcases full of books. He looks like that type of guy who wants a modern, sleek city shop with no personality. Yuck.

Carol leans over. "Looks like the guy you've been pining over the past six months finally got himself a nice little friend."

"Yeah, well, his friend seems like he has a stick up his butt," I mumble. Carol snorts with laughter as the bell rings and another customer comes in. She's definitely just passing through. I let Carol know I really am going back to the office now to do some work and storm off annoyed.

Once I'm back in my office, I set my forehead down on my desk, let out a sigh, and hope this date tonight isn't as terrible as I'm imagining. Because, honestly, I could probably use a night out. It's been a long time. It'll help me to not think about how my business is possibly going to crumble, how Liam is never going to ask me out, or how Mr. Americano seems like he is here to stay for a while and is already pissed off about something.

Later that evening, I'm getting ready for my double date with a complete stranger. That part makes me particularly upset. These guys could be completely crazy knowing Jess. I remind myself that I'm a mostly outgoing and extroverted person. I do it all the time at work. I can be nice and bubbly when I want to be. I can totally handle this.

My apartment is above my coffee shop, which closed an hour ago. Luckily, Mr. Americano and Liam were long gone when I finally came out of my back office, which left me cleaning, saying goodnight to Carol, and locking up behind her.

I laid on the couch with Trixie for an hour while scrolling my phone. I could've spent that time doing a million other things, but of course, time just seems to slip away while doom scrolling on social media.

Trixie is now sitting on my bathroom counter watching me meticulously put on my eyeliner. I absolutely loathe putting on makeup, probably even more than I hate putting my bra back on. I need both, though. On the off chance this guy is something magical, I want to at least put in a little effort. Plus, Jess might actually kill me if I don't at least give it some effort.

I hear a knock at the door. I yell to Jess, "It's unlocked, like it always is!"

Jess comes storming into the bathroom. "Why do you leave it unlocked? You are going to get yourself killed one of these days, Sarah Anne! And why aren't you ready yet?! I do *not* want to be late!"

I'm already about to lose my shit, and she has been here for five freaking seconds.

"Because I worked all damn day, and I'm doing you a favor, so sit down and shut up. I'll be ready in five minutes."

Jess mumbles, "Fine," and then proceeds to launch into great detail about the floral arrangement class she took today in Carnation Springs, a town about forty-five minutes away. Jess desperately wants to do floral arrangements for a living, but we live in this backwater town that has absolutely no use for her flowers. She's going to need to move to the city eventually; however, as of right now, she refuses to admit it to herself or me.

I look over at Jess. Gosh, my sister is adorable. Her dark hair is full of beautiful beach waves, the kind that my hair could never have. Her makeup is immaculate. Her smokey eye is one most women would kill to master, and she also has her signature bright red lipstick on, but she seriously doesn't even need any of it. Tonight, though, she has outdone herself, wearing a gorgeous red dress with a black leather jacket that gives the illusion it was custom-made for her body, and she has the cutest black heels. I, myself, would probably—*definitely*—fall over in those shoes.

I finish applying my makeup—which, unlike her, I do need—and slip on my favorite pair of shoes.

Jess makes a face as if she might vomit and then shouts, "You are wearing *those*?!" while aggressively pointing toward my shoes.

She honestly looks like the thought of my shoes alone might kill her.

"These are my favorite shoes, and I don't *want* to go on this date. So again, shut up or I'll just stay home."

My favorite shoes are a pair of Converse from two years ago. I think they look great with my jeans, which are a huge step up from my usual black leggings that have a hole in the knee.

Jess sighs. "What if this man is your future husband?"

"My future husband will adore my Converse, so let's just go now, before I change my mind." I stick out my tongue at her and grab my purse off the hook. I smirk as we head out the door. I chose my favorite purse—a sparkly pink cat face with a gold chain, and I just know she hates it.

When we finally get in the car, I ask Jess where we are going to meet the boys.

She says, "Movie theater and then Delano's."

Delano's is about the only "date" restaurant in town, and it's probably not considered a date-worthy spot by most out-of-towners.

Delano's is equivalent to an Applebee's, if Applebee's tried to be a hot date spot. There are white linens on the tables, but they've seen better days. There is "mood lighting," basically just dim lights throughout and candles on the tables. The food, though, is actually probably much, *much* worse than an Applebee's to be honest.

I peer over at Jess. "How did you meet this guy, and why are we making him suffer with food at Delano's?"

Jess sighs. "Sarah, do you want to drive forty-five minutes to another town for a date? No, I don't think so, so we are going to Delano's because it is the only way to get *you* to go with us." She stops at the next stoplight, glances over at me exasperated, and says, "I met him at the grocery store last week, and he's adorable, Sarah, so please, please, *please* be nice to him and make this work for me. I really like him."

The light turns green, and Jess looks back at the road. She starts smiling, and it's one of those *I'm in love* smiles that you see in movies. I would know; I watch a lot of movies. It's that smile that tells me she's already got it bad, so I need to be on my best behavior tonight.

After a quiet twelve more minutes of driving with Jess, we pull up to the movie theater that's just on the other end of town. Jess parks the car, and we get out. We start walking to the front door when I see Liam and Mr. Americano.

Oh god, the last thing I need is for them to see me on an embarrassing blind date. I start turning to Jess to tell her we need to hide somewhere else while we wait for her date when she smiles ear to ear, waves her hand in the air, and shouts, "LIAM!"

CHAPTER SIX

Sarah

I STOP IN MY tracks.

Oh no.

Oh nooo.

No, no, no.

Jess is smiling so big, I think her cheeks might crack open. Jess turns to me and says, "Liam, this is my sister, Sarah! Sarah, this is Liam!"

Liam turns to look at me—after admiring my sister like she's God's gift to planet Earth. *Shit*, and just like that, there goes my dream man.

I might throw up. *My* perfect man is my little sister's date, and now that I've done the math, that means Mr. Americano is mine . . .

Liam smiles at me and says, "Wow, Jess, I didn't know your sister is *the* Sarah. I visit her coffee shop every day!"

Jess smiles even bigger, which I didn't think was humanly possible, while fluttering her eyelashes up at Liam.

Her red lipstick is making her look like a freaking sex goddess. I should've known that if Liam ever met her, it would be game over for me.

Mr. Americano is staring at me and still looks like he has a stick up his butt. Honestly, what is his problem? He stares at me like I'm freaking macaroni and cheese with ketchup on it. *Disgusted*.

Jess and Liam start talking about how we should start making our way into the theater when Liam leans over. "Gosh, I'm a terrible friend. Sorry. Sarah, this is my friend Ethan. Ethan, this is Sarah. You may have seen her earlier at the coffee shop."

Ethan, a.k.a. Mr. Americano, is still staring at me with his mocha brown eyes. I'm not sure he even heard the words his friend just spoke. "Nice to meet you, Ethan!" I grumble, "Hope you enjoyed your Americano!" That second part probably had just a little too much sass and sarcasm to it.

"Wow! How sweet of you to remember his order!" Liam is practically jumping up and down. He clearly did not catch the sarcasm dripping from my voice. Liam is putting off major golden retriever energy, or maybe I just read too many book reviews. That is definitely a term the hip book people use right now. Seriously, though, Liam has just taken loyal best friend to a whole new extreme.

Liam grabs Jess's hand and starts leading her to the theater.

Just like that, my perfect man is now the *worst* possible candidate for a love match. He is officially off limits for me, and my stomach completely bottoms out as I realize, this date *just* started and we still have hours left to go.

Mr. Americano—sorry *Ethan*—has yet to say a single word to me. We are sitting in our seats now, and there are fifteen more minutes before movie time, and he hasn't even said hi or nice to meet you.

I really don't know what this man's problem is, but I can't stand to be near him right now. I lean over and tell Liam and Jess, "I'm going to get some drinks and snacks. Do you guys want anything?"

Jess asks for a small soda, and Liam says he'd love a bottled water. He tries to hand me five dollars, but I tell him to hang on to it and walk away.

I make my way out to the concession stand in the lobby. I stop to look at the menu when someone bumps into my back. I turn to apologize for my abrupt stop when I realize it's freaking Ethan.

Good lord, why did he follow me out here? I will admit that the henley shirt with jeans that he has on now is a huge improvement from the fancy man suit he was wearing earlier in my shop. Of course, he still looks hot, stubble accentuating his sharp jawline, but he's not my type. I enjoy a man with a fun personality and a good sense of humor and, therefore, a man who drinks a fun coffee. This guy screams *I like to read horror books and eat kale in my free time.*

"Sorry, I didn't realize you'd come with me," I say. When I realize I'm grumbling again, I try to speak up and speak more clearly. "Did you want something to eat?"

He finally speaks, to my utter and complete shock. "I think we are going to dinner later after the movie?"

If he is about to tell me I don't need to snack before dinner, I might punch him in his stupid, beautiful, perfect nose.

"I need to snack in movies, or I'll fall asleep. I get up early for work." I turn back around to end this conversation. I have zero interest in talking to this man any more than I have to.

Luckily, it's just in time, as the line clears, and I walk up to the counter.

"One small Diet Coke, one bottled water, one large Dr Pepper, a large popcorn, two corn dogs, Sour Patch Kids, and a blue raspberry Icee, please." I turn around to Ethan. "Are you sure you don't want anything?"

He is staring at me, and if looks could kill, this would be it. The expression on his face would be the final blow.

"Just another bottle of water, please."

I turn back around. The cashier charges me a crazy amount for my snacks and drinks. Ugh, going to the movies is seriously getting expensive.

She swipes my card, gathers all my snacks, and hands them over.

I'm honestly slightly relieved Ethan followed me out here. I probably wouldn't have been able to carry all this myself.

"Here, can you carry these?" He nods his head, which is all the confirmation I need before loading up his muscular arms with some of my snacks.

I carry the popcorn over to the self-serve center and cover it with butter and salt. Ethan's eyes tell me he thinks it's too much, but joke is on him. If there weren't other people here with me, I'd put on even more. However, just in case Jess or Liam want some popcorn, and god forbid even Ethan, I'll keep it lower than my normal amount.

We make our way back into the theater and sit down right as the trailers begin to play.

CHAPTER SEVEN

Ethan

I'M STARING AT THIS movie screen like my life depends on it.

If I look over at Sarah at all, I might lose my mind. She looks even more beautiful than she did this afternoon at the café, which I didn't think was humanly possible.

She also isn't afraid to eat whatever the hell she wants, which is a huge turn-on for me. I'm so tired of city girls and their kale salads. She might be perfect, and I'm retreating into myself because I don't know how to act. I'm super nervous.

I'm trying really hard to keep my distance and play things cool because this trip is temporary. I'm not going to be living in Daisy Ridge, and I'm not about to lead on this beautiful woman. She deserves more than a guy who is about to build competition in her little town and then bail. I don't want her to think I'm interested, even though I definitely am, and my heart is fluttering wildly in my chest because my head is fully convinced that she's perfect.

Luckily, it doesn't seem like keeping my distance will be very hard, because she seems like she has already decided she hates me.

Which I am totally fine with.

If she hates me, then there is zero chance of broken hearts in six weeks when I leave. I just need to make it through six weeks of keeping my distance and six weeks of suffering through Liam.

God, he is completely obnoxious. On the way here, he went on and on about what a "hot piece of ass" Jess was. I feel really bad for her. They clearly have two completely different ideas of where this is going and what this relationship actually is.

I keep staring at the screen. I don't even know what is happening in this movie. All I know is that I need to keep looking at it and not at Sarah.

I take a deep breath and try to unclench my teeth.

CHAPTER EIGHT

Sarah

THE MOVIE IS ALMOST over, and my drinks and snacks were the perfect appetizer. My stomach is ready as it will ever be for a crappy meal at Delano's.

I'm actually pretty happy that the beginning of this date was a movie. There was absolutely no talking required. Which was ideal, given the circumstances. However, Jess and Liam holding hands for the entire movie was a huge distraction for me.

In my weeks of pining and lusting for Liam, I never even considered he might have someone else here. I know that makes me sound super naïve. I just saw the absence of a ring on his hand and assumed he would eventually be mine. He never came in with anyone else, so I stupidly assumed he was just a workaholic loner like me.

Now that I know there is someone else *and* that someone else is my little sister, I'm trying to rewire my brain to remind myself he is completely *off limits forever* now.

To my right, Mr. Americano is being a typical "Americano man," sitting here unmoving for an entire two-hour movie. Is he actually enjoying this romantic comedy Jess picked? So much so that he can't take his eyes off the screen? I can't imagine an Americano man appreciating a fun rom-com like this.

When the movie finally ends a few minutes later, I sigh with relief. Jess and Liam look at each other and smile. Holding in a cringe, I look over, and it feels like Ethan is doing the same thing.

Liam looks over Jess's shoulder toward Ethan and me. "Shall we go to dinner now?"

"Sounds great!" I say and stand up abruptly. I grab Ethan's hand and yank him up with me. The moment I do, I realize how completely awkward that is, since we've said less than three sentences to each other tonight, max.

I let go of his hand as fast as I can, not even making eye contact with Ethan because I'm a coward in complete fear. We start heading out of the theater, Liam and Jess hand-in-hand, while Ethan and I walk awkwardly far apart. Suddenly, Jess shrieks to Liam, "YAY! You can drive my car!"

Liam turns around. "Ethan, I'm going to drive Jess's car. Sarah, you can ride with Ethan in his car." Liam looks to Ethan. "Follow us?" he says with a wink at his friend, and then he turns and walks away with Jess.

He gave approximately zero seconds for Ethan or me to object to his plans.

I glance over at Ethan, and I can practically feel the rage pouring out of him. He grunts and starts walking.

It honestly feels like I'm missing something tonight.

Why are Jess and Liam already so close? Close enough for him to drive her car? And *why* does Ethan look like he wants to rage at them? Does Ethan like my sister too?

I shrug my shoulders and glance at Ethan. "Where did you park? I can tell you directions to Delano's . . . To be honest, I don't think they are going to wait for us."

Ethan grabs my hand and starts walking us in a different direction.

Suddenly, he seems like he just realized what he did and quickly drops my hand the same way I did five minutes ago. "I'm over this way," he mumbles, still refusing to make eye contact with me.

Well, at least we have one thing in common so far. A downright hatred for this entire situation.

Ethan opens the passenger door of his car, and I find myself climbing up into a car that is not at all what I pictured for a "hot Americano man." He has an old 1996 red two-door Jeep Wrangler. It's a soft top, and I immediately want to ask him to take the top off. His steering wheel has a cover on it with faded flames up the sides, and he has a pair of lime green dice around his rearview mirror. It is not at all what I expected the suit and tie man from my coffee shop earlier today to be driving. It happens to be a car I would pick out for myself. I've always wanted a Jeep, but since I live where I work, I've never felt a huge need to buy a car.

Ethan opens the driver's door and slides in with ease. He has rolled his shirt sleeves up to his elbows now, and it takes me a minute to realize I'm staring at his muscular tan forearms.

Ethan still won't make eye contact with me, so on the plus side, I don't think he just saw me drooling over his arm muscles.

Ethan turns the key and starts the car, peers over at me, and grunts, "Where to?"

After an incredibly awkward and very silent drive to Delano's with Ethan, we show up to find the place completely *packed*. I'm shocked and confused. When has Delano's ever been packed?! The place is a pit, and no one in town is a huge fan.

The manager, Shelby, who I went to high school with, comes over. "Sarah! Oh, girl, are you and Jess trying to get a table?! Man, we are swamped! A college swim team's bus broke down on the freeway, so they *all* came here for a bite. Who knew a swim team could be this big?!" She glances around the room in awe.

I smile because our high school swim team had all of three people on it. "No worries, we can wait for a few minutes! We don't mind!"

Jess leans over my shoulder. Getting Shelby's attention, she starts pointing. "Hey! I see a couple of tables back there by the bathroom. Mind if we snag those?"

Shelby looks over her shoulder to where Jess is pointing. "Oh, those tables don't move. They are bolted to the ground because of fire access, but if y'all don't mind splitting up, they are all yours!"

Liam is practically bursting with glee. "Great! We will take them." He and Jess practically dance off toward one of the two tables.

I glance over at Ethan. "Do you want to grab the other table? Or would you rather saw off your own hand?"

Ethan shows no emotion at my sarcastic joke. I sigh and walk over to the other table. It's too far from Jess and Liam to even consider talking with them.

Sitting across from Ethan might be actual torture. Especially without Liam and Jess here as a buffer. I'm starting to think he may actually choose to saw off his hand.

We sit at our table, or what I will refer to as hell for the evening, and Ethan starts looking over the menu. I'm staring at his face because I already know what I'm ordering. I'm playing it safe tonight.

Ethan's jawline is something that should be studied . . . for scientific purposes, of course. The stubble growing across his chiseled jaw has me lost in a fantasy of thigh tickles.

CHAPTER NINE

Ethan

SARAH AND I ARE sitting at our table by the bathroom. I keep looking over the menu, but every time I steal a glance at her, she is not. She's just staring at me and seems lost in her thoughts. I guess she already knows what she wants to eat. I shouldn't be surprised by that, as I'm sure she has been here before. Also, she is definitely the type of girl who knows what she wants.

The waitress comes by and asks what we will be drinking. "Vodka tonic," Sarah says to her with a smile. She turns and is clearly waiting for me to say something.

I'm going to play it safe in a place like this, no mixed drinks tonight. "Bourbon. Neat please."

I'm not risking food poisoning from any of their mixers.

The waitress gives us a tight nod and smiles before walking off.

I finally look back at Sarah, and she looks . . . beautiful.

I am honestly so uncomfortable for so many reasons. The most persistent reason is that the whole drive over, I realized this girl is *really* going to hate me.

She has a beautiful little coffee shop in this very small town. I don't think she is going to love the idea of me building a Starbucks nearby. On top of that, she already seems annoyed with me for one reason or another.

I don't even know what to say. I can't ask her about work. I've seen her work, and she knows it. I also don't want to bring up work, because I definitely can't talk to her about my work. She will ask why I'm here, and she will hate me.

I clear my throat and set down my menu. Sarah opens her mouth, and I already know she's going to ask a question and despise me even more than she already does.

CHAPTER TEN

Sarah

I OPEN MY MOUTH to talk after a three-minute-long fantasy about his jaw. It really is truly unfair how attractive he is. I don't even know what to say to this man.

I want to shout, *Why are the handsome ones always complete assholes*? But I decide against that.

Instead, I think I will try to be brave and go for some small talk. "So what do you do for work, Ethan?"

"Uh, maybe . . . uh . . . Let's not talk about work," Ethan says gruffly, and now he's back to brooding. *Ugh.* What is with this man? He is kind of infuriating. On the plus side, him being a jerk makes it much easier to stop fantasizing.

"Uhm, okay. What do you do for . . .*'fun'*?" I put air quotes around the word fun because I have a feeling this man doesn't do anything that remotely resembles fun.

Ethan smirks. "I enjoy hiking, puzzles, eating good food, listening to good music, and occasionally running, preferably on a trail." He looks up at me over the top of his menu and smiles. Genuinely *smiles*. I didn't know his face could physically accomplish that.

But, good god, it's a good thing I don't *actually* like this guy because he has a smile that most women would swoon for. If I actually liked this man—which I don't—that smile would probably make butterflies go off in my stomach, so it's a good thing I don't . . . Right? There are definitely NOT any stomach butterflies. My stomach is perfectly fine.

"What do you do for . . . 'fun' Sarah?" He mimics the way I asked him, putting air quotes around *fun*, and now he is quickly moving back to making my blood boil.

I smile politely at him, even though I'm fuming on the inside. I hate when people mock me. "I enjoy reading, watching crappy reality TV, cuddling with my cat, romantic comedies, and of course, working."

He arches a brow at me. "Some would say working isn't fun."

I give him my best *I hate you* smile. "Some people need to find better work, then."

The waitress comes by and puts our drinks down on the table. Ethan picks his up. "Well then, cheers to doing what you love," he says with a lazy, half-assed smile.

I clink my glass with his, and down as much as possible in one sip.

I glance over, and he is also pounding his drink at an alarming rate. Boy, are we in for a *very* interesting meal.

The waitress comes back to take our orders. I order spaghetti, no meatballs. I don't trust the meat at Delano's after getting sick a few years ago. You really can't screw up pasta, though. It feels pretty safe.

Ethan orders a burger, medium with curly fries. In his head, he probably thinks a burger is a safe choice. Here is hoping he is right about that tonight.

Twenty-five minutes have passed, and we've made small talk about our hobbies and interests. When we hit an awkward lull in conversation, we started to make fun of the people surrounding us. Not on purpose—the game started out innocently enough. I said, "What do you think those people are talking about?" while pointing at the couple across the way, and he started acting out their voices and pretended to be them. I laughed, and it continued from there.

We still don't have food, but I've had two more drinks. I might be drunk, but I could just be tipsy. It's hard to tell, but we are laughing. Yep, Ethan and I are laughing *together*. If you had told me thirty-five minutes ago that we would be laughing together now, I would've questioned your sanity. But here we are, pointing at all the different people in Delano's and guessing what they could be saying.

It's been a fun game so far. I pointed to some very challenging victims, and yet Ethan has nailed them all. At one point, I doubled over laughing so hard, I cried.

When we start to run out of people to point at, I glance over to my sister, who is giggling and leaning forward toward Liam. I know exactly what she's trying to do. She's trying to make her boobs look bigger, and it's totally working.

Ugh, I *still* can't believe he is her date. I'm once again reminded of why I was in a bad mood earlier and frown. I look back at Ethan. He is staring at me with an odd, curious expression on his face.

"What do you think they are talking about?" I point over my shoulder toward Jess and Liam.

Ethan frowns. "Are you not happy that your sister is on a date with Liam?" he asks quietly, almost a whisper.

I hesitate, wondering how honest I can be with him. "I . . . uhh . . . don't know?" I scrunch up my face, trying to think about what to say next.

Ethan tilts his head slightly while he looks over at me. "Do you not like Liam?"

I'm completely distracted by his cute tilted head and sad puppy dog face momentarily that I almost forget to respond to his question.

"Uhh, no, quite the opposite." I let out a heavy sigh and decide to go with the truth. "Honestly, he has been coming into my coffee shop daily for a while now. I had kind of hoped I'd eventually work up the nerve to ask him out." I pause, looking into his eyes to see if I can find any emotion seeping through. I don't, so I continue, "Obviously, now that he is dating my sister, that is no longer happening *ever*, which is fine. It's not like I had my hopes real high or anything . . ." I glance back over at them. "I kind of feel like I missed something, though. This can't possibly be their first date. I mean, *look* at them." I nod my head in their direction.

Ethan glances over and then looks back at me. "No, I didn't gather that this was their first date." He pauses. He looks like he is contemplating his next words carefully.

He opens his mouth to say something, but our server interrupts with our food. Ethan smiles up at her and says, "Thanks so much."

She walks away. Ethan looks at me with some kind of expression I can't quite recognize. God, I hope it isn't pity. When he opens his mouth to speak finally, he just says, "Let's eat. I'm sure you're hungry."

I can't tell if he is being sincere or if he is making fun of the fact that I ate enough for all four of us at the movie theater. Either way, we begin eating in silence. This man is still such a mystery to me. Maybe I misjudged him earlier today?

CHAPTER ELEVEN

Ethan

SARAH IS FAR TOO amazing for Liam. I can't believe she just said she was hoping to ask him out someday. I don't hold it against her. This is a small town, and Liam is a handsome guy who has been hanging around here for the past six months. I'm sure that doesn't happen every day in a place like this.

And if I know Liam, he definitely didn't disclose to Sarah that he isn't moving here, that eventually he'd be leaving. So I get it.

I don't take it personally. I also don't take it to heart that she doesn't seem interested in me. I look like I'm just passing through. Heck, Liam even said I was just visiting when he spoke to Jess earlier. I can't blame her, in a town like this, where people are always just passing through, I imagine you need to hold back a lot. Make sure to not get your hopes up about the people you meet. I can tell Sarah puts a guard up.

We are eating in total silence, and I would do anything to make Sarah laugh and smile again like she did earlier, because it was radiant. It was like watching a southwest sunset on a cloudy day, full of so much beauty that you can't take your eyes away.

Her laughter made all my stress, worries, and frustrations disappear. All I could think about was how to get her to laugh again.

Now I have absolutely no idea what to say. I don't know how to get us back to laughter after her confession. I glance up at her from my dry, chewy gray burger. Apparently, a burger was not the safe choice here like I thought it was.

She's looking down at her spaghetti and twirling it around her fork. I can tell she is in her thoughts. I clear my throat, and she glances up at me through her eyelashes.

"What's your cat's name?" It's the only thing I can think of to ask right now.

"Trixie." She smiles slightly as she says it. "She's a calico I got from a rescue back when I was twenty. She is a *very* serious part of my life."

"I love that. One of my younger brothers volunteers at an animal rescue in a city about four hours from here. He loves it. Animals not having a home breaks my heart. I wish I could adopt them all, or at least one. Maybe someday when I'm not traveling anymore . . ."

As soon as that last part leaves my mouth, I realize I need to slow down. It just feels easy and comfortable to talk with Sarah.

When I glance back up from my burger and at Sarah, she is smiling, which could be the first real smile *at* me all night. Sure, we were laughing and smiling earlier, but it was at the expense of others. She looks happy about what I just said. She looks like she is *enjoying* my company for the first time this evening, and I want to relish in that feeling forever.

She sighs. "I wish I could take on more cats, but for now, it'll just have to be me and Trixie. The café is too demanding of my time, but maybe someday..." She says it wistfully, like she actually believes it to be true. She quickly changes the subject, though. "So *one* of your younger brothers? How many siblings do you have?"

"I have four younger brothers. They are all technically my half brothers, but we grew up as true brothers. My mom had me at sixteen and married their dad when I was five. He legally adopted me as his own." I realize I'm oversharing again, but I can't seem to stop with her.

"*Wow*! Five boys. Your mom must be a very strong woman. I can't even handle parenting one cat some days." She giggles, and it's one of those *I've had too much to drink* giggles with a hiccup at the end.

"Yeah, my mom is a strong woman. I don't think I could even survive half of what she has been through, but she not only survives, she perseveres." I get a little sad thinking about my mom. I need to give her a call soon and see how she is doing.

Sarah looks at me, and I see . . . sadness in her eyes. There are tears rimming her eyes, and she speaks softly. "She sounds amazing."

I reach over and grab her hand instinctively. "She is . . . What about your family?"

She takes a deep breath and removes her hand from mine. She places her hands in her lap and fidgets with her napkin there.

"I only have one sister." She gestures over toward Jess and looks her way. "We are super close, even though she drives me absolutely crazy. Our dad is awesome; he does the best he can, and we are both really close with him, but my mom . . ." Her voice trails off as she zones off.

She glances back at me, eyes locked on mine. "My mom passed away. It was a long time ago. It's still been hard on us all, but we've all adjusted well." She gives me a weak smile that doesn't meet her eyes.

"I know what that's like in a way . . . My dad—well not my biological dad, but my *real* dad in every way that matters—he passed away recently and unexpectedly . . . It's been super hard on my mom and brothers." I pause, considering my next words.

"What about you, though? How are *you* doing?" Sarah asks.

"I . . . " I pause. "I don't know. I don't think I've had time to . . . process my grief," I answer honestly. It's the first time I've said it out loud, and I feel a pinch in my chest. I miss my dad so much, but life had to move on. I had his business to run. I didn't have time to grieve the way I know I need to. I rub at that pinching sensation in my chest.

"That's . . . well . . . we'll work on that." She reaches over and grabs my hand on the table.

The food is gross, but the company is amazing. I didn't want to go on this date tonight, but I'm glad I did.

It's the first time I've felt a smidge of comfort since my dad passed.

*

CHAPTER TWELVE

Sarah

I'M HOLDING MR. AMERICANO's hand. Ew.

I'm HOLDING HIS HAND.

Why? My brain is scrambling. Somewhere between laughing about people and looking around this restaurant, hearing about his family, and the multiple drinks I've had, I think I have started to *like* him?! That can't be right, though. He drinks Americanos and he wears a Rolex. He's broody, and . . . I sound like a little girl with a high school crush saying I *like* him.

I'm comforting him. Yes, that's it. I'm just being a friend and comforting him. Holding his hand doesn't need to mean anything.

The rest of dinner passes in a flurry. Ethan and I chat about movies, breakfast foods, and whether cereal should be considered a soup. The topic obviously leads to whether a hot dog is a sandwich.

By the end of the meal, I'm four drinks deep and giddy at the prospect of watching *The Fall Guy* with Ryan Gosling in the future, because Ethan says I will love it, and I, for some reason, truly believe him. Plus, I'd watch anything with Ryan Gosling. He's the best. Have you seen him gush about his wife? Goals.

Jess and Liam leave in Jess's car. Before they take off, she gives me a big hug and tells me to get home safe. She gives me a wink when Ethan isn't looking. I gag, and she laughs. She frustrates me beyond reason, but I love Jess more than anything. I'd go to the ends of the earth for her.

This is the latest I've stayed out in god knows how long. I already know I'll be fully regretting all of this in the morning when I wake up to open the café. I will especially be regretting the alcohol because I don't typically drink this much.

Ethan and I start walking to his car.

"Sorry you got stuck driving me home," I say to Ethan as we walk across the now empty parking lot. I smile when I see his Jeep.

"No worries at all," Ethan says with a smile. "Did you get enough to eat? Want ice cream or something else to wash it all down?"

I hum at the thought of ice cream, but then I cringe slightly. "We don't exactly have an ice cream shoppe in town, but thank you for the offer! I'll eat a snack or something before bed."

Ethan chuckles softly. "All right."

The drive to my apartment is mostly quiet. There is just the soft lull of the radio station. Out in Daisy Ridge, we only get one major station. It just plays "today's hits."

"Espresso" by Sabrina Carpenter comes on, and I sing quietly in the passenger seat while drumming my hands on my thighs. I imagine this must be what it is like to be in a real relationship. The quiet moments where words aren't exchanged, but you can be yourself in each other's company.

I've always told Jess that it is the little things that make the biggest difference. The small quiet moments with our mom are what I remember most. The way she made me *feel*. The times we cuddled and watched romantic comedies, not the extravagant events she planned.

I know that is why I haven't settled for someone else. I haven't found the right person to do nothing with. Someone who I can sit in comfortable silence with. Someone who makes me feel my best.

I glance over at Ethan. His eyes are on the road, but there is a small uplift to corners of his lips, like he's happy to be in the car with me.

Maybe it's the alcoholic beverages in my system, but I can't help but like him. It's a new feeling for me. I don't think I've ever really "liked" anyone. I had boyfriends when I was younger because it seemed like I needed to. Then, after the feeling of fitting in disappeared and my business took over my life, I just haven't really met anyone who interested me enough to pursue. I've been on some dates with really nice guys over the years, but we just didn't have that spark.

In the past, I didn't get butterflies in my stomach when we pulled up to my place—like the ones I have right now. I didn't feel like my heart was going to beat out of my chest—like it is right now. I didn't have sweaty palms, or wonder whether I should invite the guy upstairs—like I am right now.

We pull up in front of my apartment, which is just the back of my café.

As much as intoxicated me wants to invite Ethan upstairs, sober me would tell me to get to bed because I need to open a coffee shop in the morning.

"I was wondering what was upstairs earlier; I guess now I know," Ethan says.

"Now you know," I repeat. "Thank you for the ride home! I would invite you in for a night cap, but honestly, I have to be up for work in . . ." I glance at the time on my phone. "Five hours, and I still need to do my bedtime routine."

As soon as *bedtime routine* leaves my lips, I want to take it back. I sound like I'm a six-year-old who needs to have a bedtime story read to me.

"Next time," Ethan says with a smile.

"Next time," I repeat back.

I stare into his eyes for probably the first time all night, and in the glow of the streetlight, I feel an urge to kiss him. I'm having an internal war with myself and remind myself, I've had four drinks tonight and now is not the time to kiss strange men. Even if they don't come around Daisy Ridge often, and even if this one happens to be gorgeous.

I decide to give him a super awkward car hug, and as soon as I do, I instantly regret it. He smells like my favorite cologne and bad decisions. His body heat brings warmth up my thighs, and I release him quickly.

I open the car door and slide out. "Goodnight, Ethan!" I close his door and walk up the stairs to my apartment. I open the door and glance back down at the street. He's still there, waiting to make sure I get inside safely. I wave and head inside.

It's like an out-of-body experience. I feel like a girl in a 90s rom-com, kicking my feet in the air and giddy. I couldn't stop smiling even if I tried.

CHAPTER THIRTEEN

Ethan

I WATCH SARAH WAVE from her door and head inside her apartment. I make sure the door is completely closed behind her before I slowly start to drive away. Tonight was not what I expected, to say the least.

I started the evening annoyed and frustrated at Liam for wanting to lead some poor small-town girls on. Let's face it, we *are* leading them on. I quickly went from annoyed to enraged that the girl I am leading on is *also* the girl whose life I'm probably about to ruin. From pissed, I moved on to utter depression, because I feel guilty about ruining her life for a job I *hate*.

However, I have to keep this deal intact. I need to get through this hellish job for my mom. She's done so much for me, and I need to do it for my younger brothers, because they deserve this business. They've worked incredibly hard for it, all of them, and they all *want* this life. The least I can do is grin and bear it, and get through the months that lie ahead. I can figure out what the hell I'm going to do with my life after that.

To make matters worse, by the end of the night, I was having *fun*. I think I have a massive crush on the girl whose life I'm currently destroying. The cherry on top is—I think she had fun at the end. Her absolutely radiant smile became more frequent, and the beautiful sound of her laugh was flowing more freely. It was an hour of my life that will forever be ingrained into my brain. It's a core memory that will now impact the rest of my existence.

I don't believe in love at first sight, but Sarah is the type of woman I always pictured I would end up with. She makes me smile. The conversation was easy, once it started. She was funny and witty, and someone I could definitely talk with forever.

Even when she seemed pissed to be with me, I wanted her to say more. There is this indescribable, magnetic pull toward her. I know I need to stay away, and that nothing serious can come from this. I just can't fight this feeling of wanting to be near her.

She doesn't know who I am, though. She asked about my job, and I skirted around the topic like an idiot. I could've told her the truth, but I didn't. It felt pointless in that moment. I'm only here temporarily, and she didn't seem interested in me whatsoever. As the night went on, though, I wish I had told her, because now . . . well, now I like her, and maybe, just maybe, she likes me too. I messed up, because now when she does find out, I have a feeling it's going to crush everything we created tonight.

I get back to the Lavender Dreams B&B, a quaint bed-and-breakfast that Liam and I are staying at while we are here in Daisy Ridge. I don't see any sign of Jess, Liam, or their car. I assume they went back to wherever Jess lives, because why would anyone want to be at this quirky floral bed-and-breakfast if they didn't have to? It honestly looks like the inside of my grandmother's china cabinet.

I take my keys out and unlock my door, flip on the lights, and start to settle in for the night. When I finally climb into the bed, I can feel the springs of the mattress digging into my back. However, I have a smile on my face anyway as I fall asleep thinking about Sarah.

Chapter Fourteen

Sarah

THE NEXT MORNING, I scrambled out of my apartment and into my café to get everything set to open. Luckily, in a small town like this, I don't have to open as early as I would if I lived in a major city. Most folks around here don't have to start heading off to work until five at the earliest. If they have to head out any earlier than that, they are probably driving to the big city anyway.

I make myself my coffee in between the first few customers that trickle in. Smithy, a regular who lives in town and runs the hardware store, comes in at 6:00 on the dot like he always does. He smiles at me and says, "Why, Sarah darling, you are beaming this morning! Did you get a good night's sleep?"

I smile back, because Smithy looks like Santa (and actually plays Santa almost every year at Christmas). Smithy is the grandfather everyone in town adores, and I will never *not* smile while looking at him.

I chuckle, and say, "Quite the opposite, Smithy. I got sucked into a double blind date with Jess last night. You know how convincing she can be. I was out pretty late, and I'm terribly tired today if I'm being honest."

Smithy's smile widens, and he starts wiggling his eyebrows at me. "A date, you say? Must be what has you grinning from ear to ear this morning!"

I laugh loudly, and clear my throat. "Was just helping out Jess! But appreciate your optimism, Smithy!"

Carol comes in for work right as Smithy is leaving. She whispers something to Smithy, and his whole face blooms the brightest red. She winks at him and heads behind the counter.

"Now, Carol, you better not be harassing any customers!" I smirk at her across the espresso machine.

Carol shouts, clutching at her chest like she is straight out of a Western soap opera and about to faint at my statement "Why I'd never!"

The next hour rushes by. It's a flurry of my regular townies and travelers stopping in on their way to a Comic-Con.

Around 7:15, Liam walks in holding hands with my sweet little sister, and I'm at war with the battling emotions inside me at the sight of them.

Jess smiles and waves from the back of the line. Luckily, they have about four customers ahead of them, so I have a few minutes to gather myself before I need to speak directly to them.

When they do finally get up to the counter, Liam orders, "Two large iced Sarah's Specials."

I glance at my sister, raising my brows in concern. Jess has never ordered a Sarah's Special, because it is flavored as her *least* favorite cookie of all time. I mean, she refuses to even make one when a customer orders it. She makes Carol or me take over so she doesn't 'gag at the smell of coconut.'

She gives me a glare back, which I know to be the *Shut up and say nothing* glare, and I want to throttle her.

I love my sister, but she's the biggest people pleaser I know, and it drives me crazy. I want to intervene here. I want to tell Liam that is not what my sister drinks, but I know Jess would be crazy upset.

It's her life, so I'll let her handle things her way.

I give Liam a tight smile. "You got it! We'll have them out soon."

I continue taking orders and making drinks. Liam and Jess are snuggling in the corner where I have a couple comfy chairs. Of course they are *sharing* one chair, which makes me completely want to barf.

They eventually leave, and things slow down. Around 9:00, Ethan walks in.

My heart instantly starts beating faster. I fumble with the vase of white lilies on the counter next to the register and pretend I am tidying up and didn't see him walk in. As if anyone could miss him. His dark hair is more relaxed than it was yesterday, not a drop of hair gel in sight. I just want to run my fingers through it.

As I fantasize about his hair, Ethan clears his throat, signaling I've been staring into the void, not paying attention.

"Hey." I smile up at him.

"Hey." He smirks back. It's almost as if he knows exactly where my thoughts just were.

I can feel a blush creeping up my cheeks and pretend to yawn into my elbow.

"Did you want a hot Americano this morning?" I say as soon as my pretend yawn is over.

"No thanks. I'll take an iced Dirty Chai and a"—he pauses and looks around the pastry case—"blueberry scone."

Well.

I don't know what to think right now. I'm at a loss for words. An iced Dirty Chai? Does he know what that is? I wouldn't have guessed it.

"Is that okay?" He looks at me with concern.

Probably because I'm standing here not moving or saying anything at all. I need to say something . . . Why isn't my mouth working? Am I having a stroke?

Carol comes up behind me and puts her hand on my shoulder. "You okay, Boss Lady?"

I nod my head in response.

"Want me to start making that Dirty Chai for ya?" I nod my head again.

Carol giggles as she walks over to the espresso machine to start Ethan's drink.

Ethan is smirking at me again, and I'm so embarrassed by this whole interaction that I think I should go back to bed for a few hundred hours.

Ethan hands me a twenty, and I finally move my hands and ring him up. I hand him his change, and finally, my mouth decides to work again. "Sorry, uh, here is your change."

Carol comes over and hands him his iced Dirty Chai. She turns and winks at me. "I'm going to take my fifteen-minute break, Boss Lady. Holler if ya need me."

"Okay!" I give her a glare that Ethan can't see.

I turn back to Ethan. "Let me grab that scone for you. Did you want it warmed up?"

"Sure, that would be great. Thanks!" He smiles at me.

It's strikingly different from the scowl he wore in here yesterday.

Is it possible I completely misjudged this man?

I warm his scone up and hand it to him. Our hands brush against each other in the handoff, and we both pull away, as if there was an electric shock at the touching of our hands.

Ethan glances down at me. "Any chance you'd want to go out again sometime? I'm only in town for a few weeks, but I'd love to get to know you more."

There it is. The other shoe.

I mean, I knew he was probably only in town for some time, but in my daydreaming and fantasizing . . . I forgot about that.

"I'd love to," comes out of my mouth before I can even process anything.

The smile on his face widens. "Awesome, it's a date. Can I pick you up tomorrow? What time do you close?"

"We close up around six p.m. tomorrow since it's Sunday," I respond.

"Great! Is seven too early?" He smiles.

"Nope, seven should be great," I say.

"Okay, I'll probably stop by for another coffee tomorrow morning, if that's okay?" he asks.

"Sounds perfect. See you tomorrow." I wave as he starts to turn and make his way to the door.

There is no one in the store now. The weather is so nice that there are a couple of people working on computers out on the porch.

Before he opens the door, he turns. "Oh! And, Sarah?"

"Yeah?"

"You look stunningly beautiful today." He smiles and walks out the door.

And I think my heart just walked out the door with him.

I glance out the window and see him climb into his Jeep and realize I definitely misjudged this guy yesterday.

CHAPTER FIFTEEN

Ethan

I'VE NEVER BEEN A guy who compliments a girl I barely know. Everything just feels easier with Sarah.

Probably because it's honest and just how I feel. I walk out to my car and get in. The ignition fumbles a little bit, but the car starts, and I'm on my way to go meet Liam at the construction site. It's about three miles from Sarah's coffee shop, and my stomach turns sour at the thought.

I asked Sarah out again because I can't stop thinking about her—her radiant smile, beautiful eyes, and our conversation from last night. But I also asked her out again because I need to come clean about my job and what I'm doing here. I know it might ruin my chances, but I want her to hear it from me and not from someone else.

I'm hoping if it comes from me, I can explain myself. Explain that I hate my job, and I'm just doing this for my family.

Although, I'm not sure that makes my situation any better, because then I'll have to admit that I'm a twenty-nine-year-old man who doesn't know what he is doing with his life when this job comes to an end.

I think that would probably be considered a red flag for most women, and I'm sure Sarah wants a man who knows what he wants. She certainly knows what she wants and doesn't hold back. She eats what she wants, says what she wants, wears what she wants—and does it all with confidence. Confidence is the sexiest thing a woman could wear.

I pull into the construction site, and Liam is aggressively making out with Jess with her pushed into the driver's side door of her car. From my point of view, it looks uncomfortable and miserable for poor Jess.

When my tires hit the dirt, they pull apart.

I park and get out of the car.

"Hey, Jess!" I smile at Jess as she wipes her mouth. The red lipstick she wears is smudged.

Jess looks so much like Sarah, it's not hard to tell they are related. Jess is shorter and smaller in stature. She also has the appearance of someone who drinks celery juice and works out one hundred hours a day. I know that's probably *not* what she does. However, fitness and health are definitely a priority for Jess. I start to wonder who they resemble most, their mom or their dad? I wonder if I'll ever get to find out . . .

The thought stops me in my tracks. I've honestly never thought about the future with a woman. I've only just met this girl twenty-four hours ago, so I need to reel it in and stay chill. This whole thing is turning into some crazy infatuation.

Jess smiles at me. "Hey, Ethan! I see you stopped for coffee." She follows her statement with a wink.

"Ah yes, I did. Wanted to get some coffee and ask your sister out on another date." I smirk at her.

Jess's smile triples in size, if that's even possible. Her eyes light up, and she jumps in the air, squealing with a sound something close to what I would imagine a pterodactyl to sound like.

"OH MY GODDDDDD!" Jess yells while jumping. "I knew you guys would hit it off!! Ugh, I can't wait to rub it in Sarah's face!"

Suddenly, it hits me that Jess is *here*. At the construction site.

"Uh, hey, Jess . . . quick question, do you know what we are doing *here*? Like at this spot?" I glance from her to Liam. Liam is looking at his phone, not even pretending to be interested in what is happening around him.

Her smile turns to a frown. "Unfortunately, I do. You told Sarah last night, right?"

I look down at these stupid dress shoes. "I, uh, well . . . "

Jess sighs. "Please tell me you did not ask my sister out on another date *before* telling her what you're doing here . . ."

"I asked her out again so I could tell her, alone and in person."

I know I'm wrong. I should've told her last night. Liam's phone starts ringing, and I watch him step away to answer it. I look back at Jess. "I had a lot of fun with Sarah, and I think . . . well, I think she's perfect. I got scared. I didn't want to ruin things last night when she had taken so long to get comfortable. She had *just* finally smiled when she asked what I did for work. I panicked. I promise I'm telling her tomorrow Jess; I just want her to hear it from *me*. So please just don't say anything until then . . ."

Jess gives me a faint smile that doesn't meet her eyes. "If she asks me, I won't lie to her, but honestly, we probably won't talk until Monday night anyway. That's when we have dinner with our dad. So until *then*, I will not go out of my way to tell her, but you tell her tomorrow. No matter what." She holds out her pinky to me. "pinky promise?"

I haven't done a pinky promise since probably fourth grade . . . I stare at her pinky for a long second. I finally hold mine out to hers. "Pinky promise."

"Great!" she says. "For what it's worth, the second I saw you, I knew you'd be perfect for my big sis. I can feel people's auras, and I just had this tingly feeling." She leans forward off her car. "Well, I'm off to get some work done of my own. Have fun at work, boys!" She tosses me a wink and blows Liam a kiss. Liam is walking back over after just hanging up the phone.

It seems she shares the same level of confidence Sarah has. It must be genetic.

Liam says, "Come on, man. Let's get to work."

Chapter Sixteen

Sarah

IT'S SUNDAY MORNING, AND the café is slow. There is a steady stream of people in and out, but it's not busy. Last night, I caught up on some much needed sleep after cuddling with Trixie and reading a new romantasy book by Jenessa Ren. It was everything I needed before tonight, because now I can't stop the butterflies in my stomach, and it's only 10 a.m.

Liam and Ethan came by together this morning to grab coffee, and I only got flustered once while engaging in some small talk with Ethan.

Carol is taking orders and making coffee now. She takes off at noon on Sundays, since the afternoons are always nice and slow. I'm cleaning tables and the glass on the pastry case, making sure this place stays as pristine as always.

Mayor Leopold walks in, clipboard in hand with his squirrel face. He reminds me of what a man would look like if he was actually a squirrel. Like if an Evil Queen punished a squirrel by making him live out his life as a small-town mayor. He comes up and leans on the glass pastry case I just cleaned, making me cringe.

"Hello, dear!" he says in his nasally voice. "I wanted to check in and see how you are handling the news?"

"WELL." I sigh. "NOT GOOD, LEO. NOT GOOD." I call him Leo on purpose because I know he hates it. I refuse to call him by his first name, Simon, and I especially refuse to call him what everyone else does, Mayor Leopold. It's far too fancy of a title for the rat he truly is.

"I know it can be hard to accept, Sarah, but you know we will all still come and support you. Change can be a good thing, too?" He moves around me to the register and orders a coffee from Carol.

I am fuming inside. The audacity of this man is astounding.

Mayor Leopold orders a coffee: black, two sugars, and cream. Which is fitting. He could just order a black coffee and add the two sugars and cream himself at our bar by the door, but nope. He needs to make sure someone does *everything* for him, always.

"I've done a lot for this town too, ya know?" I say to Leo, "I've created a stopping point and brought traffic to a lot of businesses by way of travelers. I think it's unfair to say I'm wrong for being upset."

Leo smirks at me. "It's not wrong that you're upset, Sarah, but it's wrong to be selfish. Do you not want what is best for the good of the town?" Carol has finished his coffee at this point and hands it off to him. He walks back toward me. "I think it's benefited your sister already, with that handsome Starbucks man, Liam, here to woo her."

My stomach plummets, and I feel like I hit the drop on a rollercoaster.

"I'm sorry. What did you just say?" I practically seethe at Leo. My teeth are grinding together like I'm about to break one.

"Oh dear! I . . . uhh . . . Have a great day!" Leo scurries out the front door like the true squirrel-rat-man he is.

I glance at Carol, who has the look of pity on her face, and I hate it. I don't need pity right now. I need a punching bag and maybe some boxing gloves.

"I'll be back in a minute," I mumble to Carol.

Carol says something back, but I can't hear her over my rampant thoughts.

I stumble into my back office and open the desk drawer, digging for my cell phone. I dial Jess, and she picks up instantly.

"Hi, Sis!" she sing-songs at me as if everything is perfect in her little world.

"Hi, Traitor," I hiss.

"Oh," she whispers.

"Oh? Oh?! That's all you have to say for yourself? I gave you a part-time job! I pay you to make me flowers for my café. Do you think I'll be able to keep doing that once there is a Starbucks in town? And you knew! You knew what he did, and you set me up on a stupid blind date with . . ."

Things start clicking into place. Ethan . . . wouldn't tell me about his job. "*WAIT*. Wait. Is Ethan? Are they both . . . ?"

"Listen, Sis, Ethan was going to tell you tonight on your date—which I am so excited about—bee tee dubs!" She pauses and lets out a breath. "I think you guys have really good chemistry, maybe even bed chem." She giggles. "You're like the definition of that Sabrina Carpenter song! Anyway, I think you should hear him out tonight. I think you would be surprised by what he has to say. So please, please, please go out with him tonight. Man, I'm on fire with the Sabrina references right now."

I honestly am so thrown off by her casual vibes right now, the way she is nonchalantly talking about how she is *excited* about this god-awful date tonight. Even though there are only three years between Jess and me, sometimes when she talks, it *feels* like so much more.

The more I think about her words, the madder—no *furious*—I become. I need someone to *feel* how fucking angry I am. This café has been my whole damn life. Without it, I have nothing. She wouldn't even have a job. I literally *live* here. I've done nothing but create this space and this life for myself.

"Oh, I'm going to go tonight, Jess. But no one will be happy with how things end up." I hang up the phone aggressively as if the phone is the one who has personally wronged me.

Ethan gave me his phone number this morning when he was here, so I run out to the register where the receipt paper he wrote his number on is.

Carol whispers, "You okay, Boss Lady?"

I glance over at her. "No."

I take the receipt paper back to the back room and shoot a text to Ethan.

> Hey, it's Sarah. Can't wait for tonight. Can we make a change of plans though? I'll pick you up in my car around seven. Want to show you something cool in town <3

> Hey! Sounds good! Can't wait! See you tonight! :)

Chapter Seventeen

Ethan

It's 6:55, and I'm anxious. I'm anxious because it's been a long time since I liked a girl. I'm anxious because it's the first time I've met a girl and thought, "Wow. She could be the one."

I'm anxious because I have to tell her the truth about my job and why I'm here.

I won't lie. The past two days working here in Daisy Ridge have been special. I always considered myself a city boy. I have never even considered living in a small town. Daisy Ridge is special, though, and I'm enjoying it. The people are friendly and excited to have us here. Everyone wants to chat and take time to stop and smell the flowers. No one here is in a rush.

In the city, there is a non-stop hustle and bustle. Everyone has somewhere to be. They are all in a hurry to their next stop. No one wants to stop and ask how you are. They don't care. They care about their next sale, next event, and next meeting.

Tonight, I'm wearing my most comfortable outfit: a faded Nirvana T-shirt from their 1991 tour I got at a vintage store, faded jeans, and black Converse. I'm so glad I packed this outfit last minute on the off chance I did something fun while on this work trip.

I'm also bringing my zip-up hoodie along with me, just in case it gets cold later. It's the Southwest, but it is January, so you never really know what the weather will be.

Sarah texted earlier to ask if she could drive tonight, and I was thrown off, but since I don't know the area well yet and I want to get to know Sarah better, I said yes. I want to see everything she wants to show me, assuming she doesn't hate me when I tell her about my job.

Just then, a 1969 Yellow Toyota Land Cruiser pulls up in front of Lavender Dreams. I walk out because I assume it's Sarah. I don't think anyone else would be coming out to the bed-and-breakfast that currently *only* Liam and I are residents at.

Sarah gets out, and my mouth goes dry. My heart starts racing. She looks breathtaking. It's the first time I've seen her hair completely down. She has makeup on but doesn't need it. She has a tight V-neck black long-sleeve top on with light-wash jeans and, of course, Converse. This time they are pink and match her cat purse.

"You look . . . wow," I mumble.

She bats her lashes at me and chuckles. "Oh, I'm sure you're used to girls wearing much nicer clothes than this in the city."

"Too bad they aren't half as stunning as you." The words slip past my lips before I can even stop them.

She appears taken aback by them, like my comment physically slapped her in the face.

She says something under her breath that I can't quite hear, but all I catch are the words "damn it" and "handsome."

"Hop in!" she yells.

I climb into the car.

"I love this car," I tell her.

"Thanks! It was my mom's pride and joy. She loved this car, and I love driving it around Daisy Ridge. It's perfect for me, since I don't drive . . . Well, really ever, ha!" She clears her throat. "Anyway, how was your day?"

I want to ask her more about her mom, what she was like and if they got along, but she changed the subject quickly, and it feels weird now. She seems really nervous or flustered. My hand automatically goes to her bouncing thigh.

I immediately want to take it back, but that would feel even weirder now. My body just wanted to calm her down and make her relax. I didn't even think.

I look out the window to keep from making eye contact. "Good. Yep, it was good. How was your day?"

"Oh, you know, just splendid," she snaps.

I glance over at her.

It feels sarcastic.

I remove my hand.

"Are you okay?" I ask.

"I'm great!" she grits out between her teeth.

There is a beat of silence, while I try to think of what to say next before she says, "OOOH, I love this song!" She turns the radio loud.

She starts singing along to "Bad Blood" by Taylor Swift. I sing along too because who can resist Taylor?

I recognize the way we are driving because it's the same drive I make to get to the job site. The Crew comes in tomorrow to start leveling the land and prepping for construction. I feel a pang of guilt in my stomach as I realize I need to tell this beautiful woman next to me *why* I'm in Daisy Ridge.

I reach over and turn down the music. "Hey, Sarah, I need to tell you something, and . . . "

"Shhh," she interrupts, "we are almost there!"

A few moments later, we pull into the construction site, and she hops out of the car before I can say anything.

I'm stunned. Why are we here? Is this what she wants to show me?

I get out of the car.

I realize I'm slow. Too slow. We are here because she already knows. I turn to look at her, and there is nothing but complete and utter loathing in her gaze.

"Sarah . . ."

"Save it," she says. "I asked you what you did for work the other night. You had your chance, so clearly you're trying to play me. Toy with your competition or something, I don't know! But I'm not some joke, Ethan, and I value myself too much to let you *win*," she spits with hatred dripping from her voice.

"Sarah, truly, I wanted to tell you. I was *going* to tell you tonight. I really like you. It isn't a joke. I didn't know how to handle the situation, and I did it wrong, but I can fix this. We can fix it? Let's talk tonight. I'll explain everything. I really do like you, Sarah, and your coffee shop."

"Don't speak about my coffee shop ever again. There is nothing more to say here, Ethan." She gestures between us with her hands and then turns abruptly, storms off to her car, and gets in. The car is still running, and I'm stunned. She does the last thing I thought she would do and takes off. She flips that car in reverse and leaves me in the dirt. She leaves me there, alone in the dark, in a strange town, standing in the middle of a pile of dirt.

CHAPTER EIGHTEEN

Sarah

I'M DRIVING AWAY, LEAVING Ethan all alone with his stupid thoughts, and *damn* it feels gooood.

Part of me feels a tiny bit bad, but I'm too furious to care about it. He made me some sick joke, and I fell for it. I have too much self-respect to actually go out on a second date with that man.

I keep thinking about my giddy joy after our first date, and it makes my eyes water.

My phone starts to ring, and I answer on my speaker phone and place it on the passenger seat. This car does not have Bluetooth.

Jess starts shouting, "Sarah Anne! Tell me you did not! Tell me you did not leave a man who was crushing on you in the middle of nowhere alone!"

"Oh, I did. It felt damn good, Jess, might do it to you next." It's the first time I've ever said something mean to my little sister. When we got to the age you'd start picking on your little sister, our mom died, and I just had to fill a void. I've always been nothing but kind to Jess. Right now, though, I'm just so angry. I can't think of anything but my anger.

I've spent my whole adult life building something I love, and three people just made a mockery of it and me. Jess deserves to feel my wrath right now.

"I'm probably going to say some shit I'll regret, Jess, so if you'll excuse me, I have a date with a bottle of Chardonnay and Trixie." I reach over and press end.

It takes a few more minutes, but I'm finally back to my space. The space I feel comfortable in.

I park my mom's car, climb up the stairs, open the door, and walk into my apartment. I collapse onto the couch. As soon as my face hits the soft cushions, I cry. I don't know why—I tell myself it was one fucking date. It's ridiculous. I don't care what other people think of me. Why is it bothering me that Ethan was exactly the tool I originally thought he was?

It's probably because he was the first guy I ever actually felt interested in. There was a draw, a pull, an invisible string—it felt like magic, and I realize I'm the naive girl I hate in all my favorite movies. I'm the silly girl who thinks something is bigger than it is. I'm Elle Woods realizing Warner is a dick.

I sit up.

I'm Elle fucking Woods.

I'm going to prove them all wrong.

This coffee shop is my Harvard Law School, and I'm going to succeed.

At some point, I fell asleep on the couch.

Eventually, I made it into my bed.

The next morning, I have missed calls and texts from Jess, Ethan, and Carol. Carol has probably heard about the whole ordeal by now—small-town gossip and all that.

I read her two texts first, just to make sure she isn't calling in sick to work, which, of course, she isn't.

> **10:59 p.m. Girrrrrrl, you're hot goss on the streets right now. Leaving the hot new guy in the middle of nowhere! Yikes!**

> **5:47 a.m. See you at work soon, Boss Lady! Can't wait to hear the tee! *teapot emoji***

Sweet Carol and her misuse of the word *tea,* which she will absolutely not be getting from me. It's going to be heavy business today as I figure out my plan of action.

I open up at 6 a.m. on Mondays, so at 5:50, I head downstairs and prep to open. One of the perks of living above your place of work.

Everything is set up, and a few customers trickle in, but it's otherwise slow. Prior to eight a.m., it's usually just our town regulars.

The travelers usually don't start coming in until at least eight, along with Carol, and I'm hoping to avoid any conversation with her about last night.

Jess walks in at 7:45. My anger immediately comes seeping back.

She looks adorable, like always, and is repping her signature red lipstick.

"Hi, Sis," she whispers, with a sad smile on her face. "I'm sorry. Please don't be mad. Life just ends up giving us challenges sometimes. Face every challenge head-on so you don't live with regrets. You're the one who told me that."

I roll my eyes. It's very Jess to use my own words against me.

"I'm not mad at *you* anymore, but I am mad," I grunt at her. "I'm not in the mood to talk about it yet. What do you want to drink, Jess?"

She orders her usual, an extra large iced black tea with honey and a splash of cream. I make it for her and hand it off.

"I'll see you at Dad's tonight?" She smirks at me.

"See you tonight, little brat. Love you." I blow her a kiss, and she leaves.

I'm not mad at Jess. It was a hard situation for her to be in, and maybe I still baby her a bit. I feel like I always will without Mom around.

Carol comes in a few minutes later. Today, she is wearing hot pink zebra print leggings, a black sweater, and a black headband pulling back her crazy curls. She is still rocking the same pink cowboy boot earrings from the other day. They must be her new favorite.

"Well, hey there, Boss Lady! Fancy meeting you here!" Carol winks at me. "Was wondering if you were alive and all since I never heard back from ya! Let's hear the teeee!" She makes a cup-sipping motion with her hands, and I'm embarrassed for her.

"Carol, there is nothing to talk about. A man—ah, nay, a *boy*—thought he could come to town and build a Starbucks while making a fool of me. He was wrong, and we are moving on with life. We are getting down to business because Daisy Ridge Coffee Co. needs to become better than Starbucks. I need a reason for people to come here. I need to work on some advertising and marketing. So it's business today, Carol. *Business*." I give her a stern look that means *no more talk about childish men*.

Carol salutes. "Aye, aye, Captain!"

She takes off to the back, probably for one last bathroom break before the little rush we usually get around 8:30.

The bell rings, and in walks Liam.

I can't believe I thought this slimeball was the love of my life.

It's kind of ridiculous looking at him now.

Liam has the look of guilt and slowly makes his way to the counter. He approaches timidly and whispers, "Hey, Sarah. How are you today?"

"I'm just peachy, Liam. What do you need?" My rage seeps into every word.

"Well, I was just wondering if I could grab a large iced Sarah's Special and a large iced Dirty Chai?" he asks with a shrug. It's not flattering to see Liam all scared of me. I'm five-two; really what am I going to do to him? What is he so scared of?

I type the drinks in to the register and turn the card reader to him.

"Be sure to leave a tip, Liam." I smirk at him.

Liam lets out a heavy sigh. "Thanks, Sarah. I didn't think you'd let me get our drinks."

I glare at him. "Well, that would be bad for business? Of course, I'm going to take your money. I'm going to take every single penny I can get from you while I can. It must mean something that my competition has been wanting my drinks for the past six months, huh?"

Liam puts his head down and starts to walk away. "I'll just wait over here for my drinks . . . "

"Great." I turn to make his drinks as Carol walks out from the back. She looks at Liam, and then at me.

"You good, Boss Lady? Want me to make those for you?" She glances at the cups I put out on the counter.

An idea passes through my head . . . "No, but can you make a large iced Sarah's Special with extra caramel drizzle as soon as I'm done with these." I continue to make the drinks.

"Uh, sure, Boss Lady," Carol replies.

I finish up the drinks and head around the counter to give them to Liam. When I'm a few steps away from him, I "slip" and drop the large iced Sarah's Special right on Liam's dress pants.

"Oh my goodness, Liam. I'm *so* sorry! What a horrible accident! Let me get you some napkins and a new drink! Wow! What a klutz I am today!" I really lay it on thick.

Liam glares at me. "These are new pants, Sarah!"

"Gosh, *so* sorry. I really can't believe I did that." I throw some napkins from the bar at him, and Carol comes around with the new drink.

"Well here are your drinks. Hope you have an *amazing* day, Liam." I smile at him and go back around the counter to get the mop.

It was worth it. Worth the cost of another drink and worth me having to mop. I feel a tiny bit better inside.

CHAPTER NINETEEN

Ethan

LIAM HOPS IN MY car. I parked around the corner from Sarah's shop because I knew she wouldn't want to see me this morning. As much as I really want to see her, I want to explain myself and tell her that I wasn't trying to hurt her. I know she isn't ready to hear from me yet, though.

"Looks like she gave you the drinks?" I say to Liam as he situates himself in my car. I look down at his pants. They are soaked, and the whole car immediately smells like coffee and a Girl Scout cookie.

"Uh, you good?" I ask.

"No, man. Sarah purposely spilled on my new dress pants. The bitch," he seethes.

"Hey now, don't call her that. You've been in that woman's shop for six months, scouting and drinking her coffee. She just found out you're working for the competition. She's allowed to be pissed at you, man." I feel the need to defend Sarah. I would throw drinks at Liam too if I could.

"Dude. It's a coffee shop; there are hundreds more," he says as he dabs at his pants with napkins.

Now, I'm mad for her. "It's not just a coffee shop, Liam. It's her whole life. She spends seven days a week running it. I assume she's there, open to close, every day. She lives above it, for god's sake! From what I can see, that coffee shop is all she has. You walked in six months ago, and she thought she got another loyal regular customer, and last night, she found out you've been *using* her. You've come to town to ruin the one thing she has . . . I'd throw a drink on you too, Liam."

"Dude, you've known me for years. You've known her for what, seventy-two hours? Chill, bro. You're being insane," Liam huffs.

There is no point in continuing this conversation. Liam doesn't get it. He doesn't care about anyone but himself. Hence why we are here this morning.

I told him we should just make a pot of coffee in the common room at our bed-and-breakfast, but he wouldn't have that. He needed some bullshit iced latte.

So I waited in the car. I knew it wouldn't be good to go in there, not today, while the feelings are still fresh.

"Come on, man. Just drive. I gotta go back to the bed-and-breakfast now and change my pants," Liam demands.

I start the drive back to Lavender Dreams. My feelings are a mess, and my stomach is in knots. My palms are sweaty on the steering wheel. There is a mountain of guilt and a storm of other emotions plaguing my mind.

I'm pissed she left me in the middle of nowhere last night without even hearing me out. I'm sad that I lost the opportunity to go on a date with the first girl I really felt like I could have a future with. I'm angry that I'm stuck doing this job with Liam, even though I hate it. I'm sad my dad is gone, because he would know what to do. I'm angry that I didn't tell her the truth at Delano's.

My stomach is in knots because I've made a mess of my life.

I pull into the parking lot of our bed-and-breakfast and get as close as I can to Liam's door. He aggressively gets out and heads inside to change.

As I tap my fingers on the steering wheel, I realize I need to do something, anything really. Sarah may hate me, and she may want nothing to do with me, but I need to find a way to get her to listen. If she would just hear me out, I think we could be friends, and I'd rather have her in my life as a friend than nothing at all.

When Liam gets back in the car, I ask him for Jess's phone number.

"Should I be worried?" Liam asks.

"Nah, man, not at all," I reply.

I dial her number, and it starts ringing.

"Hey, Jess. It's Ethan. I might need your help. Any chance you're free for lunch?"

Chapter Twenty

Sarah

It's time for dinner at my dad's house, and I'm honestly just praying we don't talk about my life. I don't want to talk about Ethan or my coffee shop, and I don't want to hear about Liam.

I walk up the porch steps to my dad's house. He's about a fifteen-minute walk from my coffee shop, just up the main road and then down Peachtree Lane. He still lives in the same house Jess and I grew up in. The same house my mom lived in. There are still little pieces of her everywhere. I don't think Dad can bring himself to change a single thing without her here.

I open the front door—it's never locked, even though I tell him all the time he needs to lock it, especially living alone and so close to the freeway.

As soon as I step inside the front door, my dad walks up to give me a hug and take my coat.

"Hey, kiddo, long day at the café today?" His warm smile makes all my problems melt away.

Coming home to your dad and the place you grew up is such a peaceful comfort that I will never take for granted.

My dad is in his late fifties now but looks great for his age. His dark hair is peppered with gray, and his face has a few smile lines, but other than that, he could pass for forty. Everyone in town always tells me about my great genetics.

I can't tell if their comments about family genetics are creepy or sweet sometimes.

"You have no idea, Dad." I smile back at him. "Is Jess here yet?"

"She should be here any minute, kiddo. Wanna talk about your day? My famous spaghetti and meatballs are done. Just tossed some cheese on top and threw it in the oven!" Ah, Dad's famous spaghetti. It's just a box of spaghetti noodles with canned sauce from the store and some frozen meatballs, but I appreciate him always cooking for us on Monday nights. Especially during football season, when the three of us sit down and watch Monday Night Football together.

"I'm good, Dad. I don't feel like talking about work any more today. Why don't you tell me about your day?" I love hearing about my dad's days. I always have. He works at a hospital about thirty minutes from here, and his days are much more entertaining than ours ever are.

Dad starts to tell me about a patient he had Friday when Jess runs in like Miley Cyrus on a wrecking ball.

"Sarah! Oh, Sarah! There you are!" She runs over and grabs my arm, and before I know it, she has her arms wrapped around me in a hug.

"Sarah, he broke up with me!" she cries.

"What? Who?" I ask.

"Yeah, who?" my dad butts in.

"Liam!" she yells at me.

"Oh, I didn't realize there was something to be . . . broken off?" I'm not sure of the terminology there.

"Sarah, he broke up with me for Shelby! Freaking Shelby that was working at Delano's the night of our date! She's like . . . the worst!" She continues to embrace me and cry.

I reach up and rub her back. "It's okay, Jess. He was a total jerk and a slimeball. It's going to be okay, I promise."

On the inside, though, I'm a rollercoaster of emotions. I liked Liam just a few days ago and was casually calling him the love of my life. I was able to throw that aside the second I realized Jess was dating him, and now that he just broke up with her, I remind myself he's still off limits forever. Plus, anyone who hurts Jess is on the shit list. She deserves the freaking world.

All that aside from *why* he's here in Daisy Ridge in the first place. The scumbag, although I never asked him why he was here, and he didn't blatantly ignore my question—like other people in town.

"Yeah? You think so?" She looks up at me with tears streaming down her face, her mascara leaving black smudges the whole way down.

"Yeah, babe, it's going to be fine. He didn't deserve you." I'll always comfort Jess, even when she's completely wrong, or, in this case, insane.

There is a long moment when no one speaks, and finally, Dad breaks the silence. "I'm going to get dinner out and start putting it on plates. You girls want to put the game on?"

"Sure, Dad. I got it!" I look at him, and we share a look. Neither of us is very good when it comes to Jess and her emotions. Mom was amazing, of course, so I try to remember what she would do. Hence why I'm currently scratching small circles into Jess's back and telling her he doesn't deserve her.

Jess takes a step back and looks up at me.

"Sarah, would you . . . would you . . . date with me?" she asks.

I'm sorry, what? What did she just say?

"I don't think I heard you right?" I say. "I think you said you wanted me to date with you?"

"Oh, I do!" Jess squeals. "Oh, Sarah, a few weeks ago, I signed up for this city date thingy. It's so cute; you'd just love it. Well, anyway, I signed up, and then I started dating Liam and . . . well, I panicked so I changed my registration to you. I figured I'd surprise you with it, but now—well, now I need my own again. So I thought I'd register myself, and then we can both do it together! Eeeek!" she squeals. "Oh please, Sarah, it'll be the most fun!"

"I'm sorry, Jess. I'm trying to keep up here—you signed me up for a dating thingy? What exactly is a thingy? Like an app? I've already done that, and I'm not really up for that again . . ." I shiver, thinking about the one and only time I did a dating app before. The horrible dates, the creepy messages, just no—I'd rather be alone forever.

Jess grabs my hands and pulls me closer. "First of all, Sarah, I *need* this. I don't want you worrying about me, but I'm struggling right now. Second of all, it's not an app. It's adorable—let me tell you all about it." She pulls me over to my dad's couch, and we sit down together.

I grab the remote and put the football game on for my dad.

Dad shouts from the kitchen, "I can hear the game. Thanks, girls! Dinner will be ready in five!"

I smile at the kitchen door, because our dad is the best. I look back at Jess, and she looks . . . whimsical. She has this far-off look on her face, and her one eye is rimmed with a tear that doesn't fall. She rapidly blinks it away. "Sarah, it's so cute. This adorable bookshop in Rose Point is setting it all up. My bestie, Lindsey, owns it— Do you remember her? You loved her! Anyway, she owns the bookshop and sets this cute thing up. You fill out a form with your interests, values, and what you look for in a partner. Then they set you up with a pen pal. For one month, you just write back and forth with some handsome stranger, and then at the end of the month, you set up a date in Rose Point. It sounds absolutely adorable!"

"Jess, what if we write back and forth for a month with a psychopath? Or a serial killer? I've read dark romance books, Jess!"

And what I don't say is that I really don't have time for this! It sounds like more work than it's worth, and I have to worry about making my business better than Starbucks.

"Sarah, you'll come up with a million excuses, but I need this, and I need you to do it with me. It'll be fun, and it's totally safe. They check everyone involved, and when you meet, it's in a public, safe place. You let them know where and when you're meeting. It's safe, Sarah; just please do this with me!" she pleads.

"Jess, you're such a brat. Fine, I'll do it, but if I'm not feeling it or if I get too busy, I am *not* making this a priority. Do you understand? I will quit if I'm annoyed with this guy," I tell her.

"*Yes*! Oh, thank you, Sarah! Seriously, you have no idea!! I'm so stoked, we are going to have the best time with this! Eek!" she squeals.

"Dinner is ready! Grab the TV trays!" Dad yells.

I get up and get our TV dinner trays. There are still four, and we all have our own color tray. No one has used Mom's since she passed, and every time I reach for mine and I see hers sitting there next to it, my heart twinges.

Mom would be happy I'm making this effort, and she would be even happier that Jess and I are going to do it together.

CHAPTER TWENTY-ONE

Ethan

I'M STANDING AT THE job site with Liam this morning. I convinced him to forgo coffee at Sarah's, and he is incredibly grumpy because of it. He's addicted to her coffee and won't admit it yet.

I'm drinking the shitty coffee I brewed in my room at the bed-and-breakfast out of a tiny Styrofoam cup. The men are here preparing the job site and getting everything ready.

I hate this job; I hate standing around here, observing. I'd honestly rather be building than just managing people here. I'm the kind of person who wants to work with my hands, and supervising others is not my forte.

My phone rings, and I answer it, "Ethan Stone speaking."

"Hi, it's Jessssss!" she practically sings into the phone, "and I have the best news."

"She agreed?" I whisper into the phone.

"She agreed!" Jess shouts. "Now listen, I'm going to meet up with you later so we can hash this out, but you can't tell her your name. Come up with a username and make a Gmail account with it. I'll handle the other logistics! Got it?"

"Yes, ma'am. Got it!" I smile into the phone.

The idea is crazy. Completely insane.

When Jess and I tried to come up with a way for me to talk to Sarah, we went through a million options. The conversation turned, and we talked about things Sarah loves. Jess told me that Sarah's comfort movie is You've Got Mail. We both paused, Jess smiled, and the idea was born. I want to talk to Sarah, I want to explain my story, but I know she doesn't want to hear from *me*. I'm not going to lie to her; I'm just going to tell her everything, the truth without her knowing it's me. We won't share names, just usernames.

This is going to work.

It takes a lot of lying and manipulation on Jess's part. I asked Jess if she was sure she wanted to do this a hundred and nine times.

She was adamant that this is what is best for Sarah, and she will always do what's best for her, whether she likes it or not.

So here we are scheming. I'm going to be her pen pal so she can get to know me . . . without knowing it's me.

I still can't quite figure out why I'm willing to go to such lengths for Sarah. We can't have a future. I can't live here in Daisy Ridge, but I like Sarah. At the very least, I just can't have her hate me. I just want her to know me and understand I had to take over my dad's job, but this isn't who I really am.

I'm not going to read into it; I just . . . want to talk to Sarah.

I hang up the phone with Jess and keep working throughout the morning with Liam. It's brutal, but it has to be done.

When I finish that afternoon, Jess meets me, and we get to work. I set up an email address: chaiguy87@gmail.com, and I'm ready to write my first message to Sarah . . .

Dear Coffeegal13,

I can't believe I'm doing this. I've honestly never done anything like this. I'm a little nervous, so forgive me if this first message isn't the best.

I'd love to introduce myself, but I'm having a hard time since I have to exclude my name and profession.

Here is what I will say, I'm twenty-nine, and to be honest, I still don't know what I want to do with my life. I worked in a coffee shop up until about seven months ago, and I loved it. Most people think that's not enough for an almost thirty-year-old man, though. However, I was happy with the way life was.

I have four younger brothers, an amazing mother . . . and I had a wonderful father. He recently passed away. I had to leave the job I enjoyed and take over this business. I currently need to keep it successful and afloat until one of my younger brothers can take over. I hate it. I hate the job, I hate the position I'm stuck in, and I hate what it has left me with.

My hope is when my younger brother can finally take over, I can figure out what I want. Honestly, though, as much as I hate this job, I'm even more terrified for that day to come. The day I need to decide what's next.

I'm single, and I've never minded that. I want to find the right person. I'm not someone to settle.

A new friend of mine convinced me to give this a try. I'm not a writer, but I'm going to try my best and give this my all.

I owe it to myself to give something in my life 100 percent right now. I feel like I've been living at 50 percent since my father passed.

I can't wait to hear from you. What you love, what you dream of—please share it all. Even if this doesn't end in a relationship, I'd love to be a listening ear for the next month.

From, Chaiguy87

I press send. I really don't know what I'm doing. I'm oversharing, and I'm not myself. I hope she doesn't think I sound like some depressed freak.

CHAPTER TWENTY-TWO

Sarah

IT WAS A LONG day at work. A kid threw up in the café after being in the car for too long. A traveler yelled at me for not having goat milk. Carol had to leave early because she started feeling sick.

So when I got home, I took a long hot shower and spent some extra time on my skincare routine. I've got background music on and my book ready. I'm about to pour myself a glass of wine, snuggle with Trixie, and have myself an incredibly relaxing night.

All of a sudden, I get a text from Jess.

> Did you get your first message? I did! Hope yours makes you smile! Can't wait to hear about it! <3

Damn it. Just damn it.

I was ready to relax. Now I need to find my laptop, read this silly letter, and *somehow* find a way to respond to it.

This is exactly why I didn't want to do this with Jess. I knew it would feel like work. I already have plenty of work in my life. I don't want more of it. It's part of the reason I don't care about dating. First dates are work—dressing up, making small talk, trying to make decisions, and trying to impress someone you don't know—it's *work*.

Although, looking back on my blind date with Ethan—once I had a couple of drinks and we laughed at the expense of others—it didn't feel like work. It felt natural chatting with him. Unfortunately, he's an absolute dick, though, so I won't date him ever again.

"Stupid jerk," I mumble as I pet Trixie.

I finally find my laptop. I gently fling it onto my couch as I head to the kitchen to get my glass of wine. As I start to get comfy on the couch, I set my wine next to me on the end table just as Trixie jumps up and curls up in my lap. Her purr makes me want to snuggle and ignore this silly message thing, but I promised Jess.

I pull open the goofy email Jess set up for me—coffee gal13@gmail.com and notice I have two new emails. One is a welcome email from Lindsey at Rose Point Books. I vaguely remember meeting her a while ago when she briefly lived in Daisy Ridge but mostly just know her from pictures Jess posts when she goes to Rose Point.

Lindsey, much like me, opened her own business pretty young. So I also agreed to do this silly thing because I know it probably helps her business in some way. The idea is pretty good, too. If we had more people in Daisy Ridge, I would consider doing something similar, but there aren't that many young singles in this small town.

The welcome email just goes through some basics—no names, no exact locations, and no professions. You can only give exact locations in one month when it is time to meet up for the date.

My stomach does pancake flips at the thought of meeting a total stranger in a month. I won't even know what this guy looks like.

I skim the rest of Lindsey's email and move on to the next. It's from Chaiguy87, and I can already see why they paired me with him. The usernames alone make for a great storyline. The subject line reads *Nice to meet brew,* and I chuckle, points to him for being punny.

I read the email, and then I read it again, and honestly, I read it a third time because it's not what I expected.

It's genuine and heartfelt. It opens up in a way I didn't expect someone would on a first message to a stranger. Mentioning the loss of his father pulls at my heartstrings. The loss of a parent is hard to process, and it doesn't seem like he has yet.

I think about my brief conversation with Ethan from Delano's when he mentioned something similar. A lump rises in my throat, but I fight it down. I will not feel sad about Ethan. I *hate* Ethan.

I look back at the email and finally hit reply. I stare at a blank screen for a while, not sure what to say. It's been a long time since I've just . . . wrote.

I decide to text Jess back first:

> **I enjoyed the first message more than I thought I would, but I don't know what to say back. What did you say?**

I take a sip of my wine, and stroke Trixie while I wait for her to reply. It's been a long time since I've talked to someone other than Jess, and even with Jess, I hold back sometimes. Not on purpose, but Jess is my little sister. I have to keep it together and be strong for her. I can't share every thought and emotion with her.

I think about my mom and dad when they were together. They had so much love for each other, dancing around the kitchen. My mom would giggle and Dad would dip her. Jess and I would giggle, too. They would kiss and we would yell *Ewww!* as loud as we could.

Those brief little memories I have are incredibly special to me. Even though my mom wasn't around for most of my life, she still gave me a picture of what true love should look like. I'm extremely grateful for that.

Jess finally texts back:

> **Sarah, just be yourself. Don't ask me what I said and don't overthink it. Talk about yourself confidently, like you'd talk about me or your coffee shop. Don't hold back. Be proud of yourself and own it. Tell him what a badass you are.**

I take a deep breath and start to type.

Hi Chaiguy87,

This is very new for me too. I don't do dating things, to be honest, I don't date. This is way out of my comfort zone. I agreed to do this with my younger sister. I love my sister more than anything.

Our mother died when we were super young, so I've felt the need to be a mother figure to her. To protect her and be there for her, anything my mom would've done for her, I try to do.

So I definitely understand doing something you don't want to do for your family. I'd do anything for my sis.

Other than my sister, I have a cat who is my baby. I love reading books, drinking wine, listening to music, and watching movies. Since I can't tell you my profession, I will keep it simple and say I own a business. My business takes all of my time. Hence why I don't date much. I work seven days a week and my business is my pride and joy. I've worked a very long time to make it successful.

You could probably guess what my business is based on my username. Let's just say I am very intrigued to hear you used to work in a coffee shop ;)

I've been a little lost lately. I recently felt pretty betrayed and angry. I'm currently honing that energy into finding a way to make my business bigger and better.

Anyway, I think I've over-shared enough for tonight. I haven't typed for a non-business reason in a really

> *long time. I kind of enjoyed this. So even if you end up*
> *being a serial killer, this was a small amount of fun.*
>   *TTFN,*
>   *Coffeegal13*

I press send, and decide I don't want to read after all. I'm too exhausted. Picking Trixie up, I head off to bed only to dream of rich dark brown eyes full of desire, strong hands in my hair, and gasps of pleasure bouncing off the walls. I wake up hating Ethan even more.

CHAPTER TWENTY-THREE

Ethan

I WAKE UP TO a response from Sarah, and I feel like an idiot, because I'm so excited to read it. I'd say I'm like a high school boy getting a message from his crush, but I don't think even that accurately describes the tight feeling in my chest this morning.

I decide to wait until after I survive the day with Liam before I read it. It's going to be a long day, as the prep work is officially finished and we are going to start the actual build. This gives me something to look forward to and helps get me through the day. I head over to meet Liam out front, like I do every morning. He is standing out there texting on his phone, like he always is. He glances up and nods his head at me. "Morning, man. Another glorious day in Daisy Ridge, eh?" His voice is dripping with sarcasm.

"It's another morning all right," I mumble, half awake. "Wanna brew up some coffee in my room or grab some from the pot in the lobby?"

Both options are terrible, but that's all I got right now.

Liam's face twists in disgust. "I was thinking we could try . . . Sarah's?" He grits his teeth together as he glances over and shrugs at me apologetically.

"Man . . . I don't know. Remember what happened last time?" I gesture my hand at his pants.

His face turns red. "I know, man, but it's the only coffee around that doesn't make me want to vomit, and I need coffee, man. I'm an addict, and I'm getting headaches." He rubs at his temples. "I have extra pants in the car, man, let's just try. She said last time she wouldn't refuse my money."

It's smart really. She should be taking our money for as long as she can. I know our two cups of coffee won't make a difference for the loss of business she may see months from now, but it's smart of her not to turn away the money of her enemies.

Unfortunately, Jess says Sarah refers to us as her arch-enemies.

"Fine," I grunt, "but if things go sideways, it's on you. I don't want to hear a single complaint."

"Yes! I'll drive, man—hop in!" Liam takes off for his car, which is parked right next to my Jeep.

I climb into the passenger seat. Liam turns on the radio and starts obnoxiously singing along to Celine Dion as we head to Daisy Ridge Coffee Co. I think about how perfect her shop is the whole way there. I can't help but wonder if she's ever thought about expanding and maybe opening a second location in Rose Point or Carnation Springs. It would definitely help with the upcoming changes.

She could also invest in some highway billboards with pictures. I'm sure a lot of women would love to stop at Daisy Ridge Coffee Co. on their travels if they knew it was coming up along their route.

Of course, I'm not going to give her any unsolicited advice. She is a smart woman who has made a successful business on her own and is capable of anything. I just can't help but feel like I want to be a part of it.

I realize as we walk into Daisy Ridge Coffee Co. that for a small-town shop, it's pretty busy on a midweek morning. Sarah looks like she is working alone, but she is keeping up. Taking orders, making drinks, smiling and laughing with what I can only assume are the regulars. We get in line. There are about three people in front of us.

Jess walks in behind us. "Mornin', gents." She nods at us and makes a beeline for the counter. She walks behind the counter and throws on Carol's apron. She ties it tight behind her, throws her hair up in a high ponytail, and walks to the back for a minute.

Sarah shouts, "Thank you, Jess. You're an angel!"

Jess walks back out. "Sorry, I was just washing my hands. I'm reeeady to paaaaartyyy!" And I immediately recognize the quote from Bridesmaids. To be honest, watching that movie was the last time I laughed so hard, I cried. It's a good one. I chuckle at the reference, and the sound makes Sarah look my way.

Her eyes lock on to mine, and I hold my breath, waiting for her reaction

She smiles in an almost sinister way. "Oh goodie, my enemies are here again!" She glares at me before glancing at Liam. "Oh, Liam, I'm *so* sorry about your pants the other day. Hope they are okay? Did you need them dry-cleaned?" She smirks at Jess.

Jess giggles as she rings up the person at the front of the line.

Sarah puts a drink on the counter. "Oh, Smithy! Your drink is ready!"

A man who looks alarmingly like Santa heads to the counter looking as jolly as can be. "Why thank ya, Sarah! Where is my dear, sweet Carol today?" His cheeks turn red.

"Oh! I'm not sure she'd want to be referred to as sweet." She wiggles her eyebrows at him. "But, sadly, she is down with the flu. I'm sure she'll be back on her feet soon. You know Carol, she can't stay down for too long!" She laughs at him, and it's sincere and beautiful.

I want another laugh like that directed at me.

"Oh, don't I know it!" He winks at Sarah, and she fakes a gag and then starts laughing again.

"Don't worry, Smithy! Jess is helping me out until Carol is feeling better! When I talk to Carol, though, I'll tell her you asked about her." She winks at him, and a blush creeps up his neck to match his rosy cheeks.

"You have a magical day, Miss Sarah!" He waves and heads toward the door.

"You too, Smithy!" Sarah beams at him with her radiant smile. I'm instantly jealous, wishing she would smile like that at me again.

We are next in line, and watching Sarah make drinks is magical. She moves with grace like she has made every move a thousand times and could make all these drinks in her sleep.

She talks to every customer and asks them about their life, even the travelers. She isn't overbearing about it, though. She acknowledges them, making sure they feel seen and heard. I can tell she can sense when they don't want to chat, though, and she leaves them be. It's amazing to watch her work.

We finally get to Jess, and she gives Liam an odd, tense look with her eyes. As if she is urging him not to say something or trying to get him to be quiet.

My confusion must be written on my face because they both look over at me, wipe the weird tension away, and immediately start smiling.

"Mornin' again. Liam, did you want your Sarah's Special?" My eyes dart to Sarah, and I can see her shoulders tense.

"Oh. Yes, please. And hey, beautiful, listen . . . " He leans in, elbow on the counter and angles toward Jess. " . . . about everything, we can still hangout. Ya know? Go to movies, eat dinner, and stuff." He tosses a wink at her.

I can't bear to watch whatever is happening here, so I interrupt. "Can I have a caramel latte with an extra shot of espresso, please?"

Jess throws a grateful glance my way.

Sarah peers over her shoulder at me. "You didn't like the chai?"

"Oh, I loved it! It was great. I just enjoy mixing it up. I get bored." I shrug.

"Hmm." She turns back around and continues making drinks.

We pay for our drinks with Jess and move to wait for them to be made.

I continue to watch Sarah move, and I can't help but fantasize a little bit about her hands. The way she grips the milk frother to clean it sends a wave of heat through my body. I look back at Jess, who is staring right at me. She winks.

I'm immediately embarrassed. I feel like a teenage boy who was caught looking at my friend's sister at school. I decide to look at my feet for the remainder of my time here. Sarah eventually calls our names, and I walk up to grab my drink. "Thanks, Sarah." I dip my head and turn for the door.

Jess abruptly says, "Thanks for coming to Daisy Ridge Coffee Co.! Hope to see you both again real soon!" She waves at us robotically, as if she is being forced to say that to everyone.

"Have a *great* day, boys!" Sarah shouts sarcastically.

Liam and I head out to the construction site, but my mind is in a coffee shop a few miles away with a pair of gorgeous brown eyes the whole time.

After a long day bickering with Liam and trying to get my guys focused on construction, I'm ready to read my email from Sarah. I read it as I eat my TV dinner alone. I had to awkwardly carry it up from the microwave in the common room because they don't have microwaves in each room at this silly bed-and-breakfast.

I have to read the email a second time because . . . It worked? She's opening up to me. She's sharing things with me. I type out my reply:

> *Dear Coffeegal13,*
>
> *I solemnly swear I will pretend I don't know your profession based on your hints. If Rose Point Books comes for me, though, I may cave. I won't lie, I don't do well under pressure.*
>
> *I'm very sorry to hear about your mother. I'm sure she was a remarkable woman, and I'm very sorry for your loss. I'm sure she would be so proud of you today, not only for creating a successful business but also for putting yourself out there.*

I don't want you to ever think you are oversharing in our emails. That's the purpose of this situation, I think. So many people just tell someone what they think they want to hear on a first date, instead of being honest about who they are. People go a few months of dating before they share any kind of emotion with the other person. Not saying they did it wrong, but I think the foundation of anything starts with friendship. So treat me like a friend. Tell me everything you would say to them.

I truly want to hear it all: your rants, your hobbies, your hopes and dreams, your secrets, and your thoughts. ALL OF IT.

So tell me more. Tell me more about your cat. What is your cat's name? What kinds of books do you enjoy? What is your favorite book? What kind of wine do you drink?

As for your recent feelings of betrayal. You are allowed to feel however you feel, and if the healthiest and best option for you is to put that energy into your business, I think that is something you should absolutely do.

So what's your plan? How are we making your business better? I know you can't share details, but I'd love to help. I would be thrilled to help you achieve all of your dreams.

I know we just started talking, but I've been feeling lost lately, too. I don't know what's next for me, and I think it would help me to help someone else figure out what's next.

I'm glad you decided to take a leap with your sister and do this email thing. I was truly so excited to read your response, and I'm already looking forward to the next!

-Chaiguy87

Chaiguy87,

Sorry for the late response. It was an insane day. I only have one full-time employee for my business, and she was out sick.

So anyway, I think you're right. Sharing with a stranger in this way is somewhat therapeutic. I don't know you, so I don't need to worry about your judgment or what you might think.

Not that I care with most people, but it's nice to kind of have that outside point of view on life.

My mom was amazing, and I know she would be proud. I think she would be disappointed in my lack of dating, but you're right. She would be proud I'm sitting here doing this.

My cat's name is Trixie. She is a calico rescue, and I adore her. I wish more people would rescue animals. I enjoy a huge variety of books. My favorites are probably romance, fantasy, and mystery. I definitely read a little bit of everything, though. My FAVORITE book is so tough. What a question! Picking a favorite feels like a betrayal to all my other favorite books. It's like a parent picking a favorite child.

I will say my most RECENT favorite was probably Heir of Sun and Moon by Jenessa Ren. It is a beautiful Rapunzel retelling with romance, betrayal, fantastical worlds—all the good stuff! I typically drink chardonnay, but I'll take any white I can get when it comes down to it.

For my business, my next focus is marketing. I'm off highway 68, and I want a sign heading each direction about five miles before my exit. Something geared toward women and mothers showing that my business is family friendly and a good stopping point on their travels. I also want to focus on my social media and make some content of my business—featuring it as a tourist destination. I'm considering inviting some influencers or travel bloggers to come in and seeing if we can spread the word that this is a great place to stop.

Anyway, what about you? Got any pets? Preferred beverages? Hobbies? Favorite books? Tell me more!

TTFN! Coffeegal13

CHAPTER TWENTY-FOUR

Sarah

I WAKE UP FEELING like I've been hit by a fucking bus.

My stomach is cramping, and my body is sweaty and freezing at the same time. My head has so much pressure, it feels like it's going to explode. All I want to do is sleep. I stand near the bathroom, just in case, and quickly shoot a text off to Carol.

> Feel like hell, please tell me you're feeling better? *prayer hands emoji*

> I am, need me to come in earlier?

> If you can, it would be amazing. I owe you one.

> doll, you don't owe me shit. I'd do anything for ya.

I shoot off a text to Jess too.

> Any chance you can help again to-day? *prayer hands emoji*

> Already on my way *kissy face*

> You're my favorite sister, you know that?

> *eye roll* Is Carol still sick?

> No . . . it's me *crying face*

> Oh shit.

> See you soon xoxo

I get ready as best as I can, head down to unlock the café, and start my opening tasks. I'm shivering, teeth chattering, and the pressure in my head is unreal.

In the years I've had this café open, I can count on one hand how many times I've been sick. Back then, I had another employee, Jill, who could help too. Jill recently moved to New York, though, to pursue her dreams, so I'm panicking thinking about how today might play out.

Will Carol and Jess be able to do this? I'm probably going to have to fight through this feeling and just work today.

Jess gets to the café about ten minutes after I've opened. I had two customers in the first ten minutes, and I couldn't tell you who they were or what they ordered. I feel like a zombie. I don't know what's happening. I really do think my head might explode. I already feel like I'm underwater.

Jess takes one look at me, and her face scrunches with disgust. "Good heavens, you look atrocious!" she shouts.

"Thanks, Jess; you're a doll." I deadpan.

"You need to go upstairs and rest!" she tells me.

"I can't. You don't know how to make drinks. I'll be fine. I promise." I try to smile at her and wobble slightly. I grab on to the counter near the register so she doesn't notice.

Jess glares at me with a menacing stare. "When Carol gets here, you go upstairs. Understood?"

I take one hand off the counter and salute. "Yes, sir. Can you run the register please? I'm going to run to the bathroom super fast."

I literally run to the bathroom and splash water on my face. I'm sweating now, and I know I probably have a fever. It's a horrendous time to be sick. I'm trying to make my business better, not have it crash and burn because of an unexpected illness.

I just hope Carol is back to 100 percent when she comes in today. I run back out just in time for another customer to walk in. Jess takes their order, and I breathe in through my nose and out through my mouth. I'm repeating the recipe to their drink in my head over and over so I don't mess it up.

My head is pounding.

I get through the next few customers and their drinks when Carol finally arrives. She is sporting a pink velour tracksuit today and comes straight back behind the counter. As she throws her apron on, she says, "Sarah, I mean this so sincerely, ya look like death, hun. You need to go upstairs and rest it off. I'm telling ya. I slept nineteen hours straight with my oil diffuser on, and now I'm good as new!"

"I can do this, guys. I've got this. I need to be down here." The last word slurs out of my mouth as I fall slightly. I brace myself on the counter as Jess and Carol share a look.

Jess comes over and grabs my arms. "You don't have this, and that's okay. Carol and I know what this café means to you. We've. Got. This. I promise. I'll run the register; Carol will make drinks. You need to rest." She squeezes my arms, just like our mom used to do.

My eyes water. I'm feeling tired and emotional. "Okay," I whisper.

Ethan and Liam walk in, and Jess turns toward them, letting go of my arms. I lose my balance, and the last thing I remember is Ethan reaching for me.

Goosebumps pebble across my skin as Ethan rubs his massive hand up and down my arm in slow, calming circles.

I look up at him. He locks eyes with me and whispers, "I knew you wanted this, too," before pushing me into the wall and kissing me.

His hands run up to my face as he cradles it, kissing me even more passionately. He presses his erection into my abdomen.

He runs one hand down my body before shoving his hand down my pants. I gasp against his lips. His other hand wraps around my neck, giving a small squeeze, just as his other hand moves inside me.

I moan.

I wake up in my bed drenched in sweat. I rip the covers off. I'm still fully clothed, and I'm so disoriented and confused. I look around the room. What the hell is the time? I glance at my nightstand, and my phone is sitting on top. I reach over, and my body aches. My arms feel like they weigh one hundred pounds. I pick my phone up and check the time.

Shit. It's almost noon. What the heck happened? What the fuck was that dream? The last thing I remember was standing in the café . . .

I leap out of the bed and rush out the door and down the stairs. I'm suddenly shivering, even though I have a sweater and pants on. Is it that cold outside? I run around to the front of the café. There is a fucking bus outside; I rush inside. It's packed, every table is full, and dear god, it's too much for Jess and Carol.

"Jesus, Sarah!" Jess shouts. My eyes dart behind the counter. I think I'm hallucinating, or maybe I'm still asleep? Am I dreaming? Ethan is behind the counter making coffee with Carol. He has his henley shirt on from our date night, the sleeves pushed up just shy of his elbows. His arms are strong and tanned; he's moving around slinging coffee like a natural.

I'm dreaming again, right? Right?

"Sarah Anne, get back upstairs *now*. We are fine." She is shooting daggers at me with her eyes.

Ethan glances over his shoulder at me. His shoulders are broad and muscular, and I feel like I might be drooling a little bit. I reach up to wipe at my face and rub at my eyes. I'm delirious, and I don't know what's happening. Suddenly, I'm walking toward the counter. It feels like I'm floating. Jess comes around and stops me.

"Please don't make me have Ethan carry you upstairs again. That was so embarrassing for you, Sarah. Go upstairs and sleep. It's busy, but we've got this. I promise. Ethan is amazing at making drinks." She gestures over her shoulder to where Ethan is.

I blink at her. I truly feel like I'm having an out-of-body experience. I glance over Jess's shoulder at Ethan. He winks at me. "You good? Or do you want another lift?" I feel the heat crawl up my neck, and I know my cheeks are probably rosy red.

I reach down and pinch my arm. Nope. I'm not dreaming.

"I'm good," I mumble.

I stare for another minute as Ethan starts making fucking latte art on top of someone's drink. It's like perfect? I blink a few times, thinking maybe I'm hallucinating from my fever . . . But he's still there making beautiful art.

Customers are eating it up. One girl is literally cheering for him.

"Sarah Anne," Jess grits out through clenched teeth. "Go *now*." She aggressively points toward the door.

I turn around, and when I get to the door, I take one more look over my shoulder. It's an incredible view to see a man like that make coffee so effortlessly. I turn back around and drag myself back upstairs.

I take a cold shower, get into some comfy pajamas, and face plant onto my bed. I have a few more fever dreams of Ethan making me an iced latte and then lifting me up onto the counter in the café and doing a lot more than just brewing coffee.

CHAPTER TWENTY-FIVE

Ethan

Coffeegal13,

Hope your employee is feeling better!

Now it's my turn to apologize for a late response, my day took quite the turn. I ended up doing something fun and exciting when I was supposed to be working. I paid for that at work later.

Trixie sounds like a cutie. I wish I could adopt an animal, but right now I travel too much for work. I'm hoping when I'm done with my current job, I can rescue something. I also wish more people would rescue animals.

I don't typically read; I'm more of a TV before bed kind of guy. I've been watching House of the Dragon lately. I definitely understand not being able to pick a favorite, though. I couldn't pick a favorite movie or TV show if my life depended on it.

I'm looking up Heir of Sun and Moon by Jenessa Ren right now. I may need to give it a try. If you love it, then it must be good. ;)

I think marketing is make or break for a good business. An exit sign would definitely draw attention. Social Media always helps as well. Do you currently have a social media presence?

I love drinking whiskey neat on the rare occasion I drink. I also enjoy a crispy Diet Dr Pepper here and there. Mostly, though, I just drink water and coffee. I like to mix it up and order different coffee drinks based on my mood.

I also enjoy hiking and biking when I get a minute to myself, but other than that, I'm a pretty boring guy.

—Chaiguy87

PS What is TTFN?

YESTERDAY, I SPENT HALF the day working in Sarah's café. Liam and I walked in to Sarah fainting; luckily, I was close enough to catch her before she hit the hard floor.

After I caught her, Jess asked me to carry Sarah upstairs, since she and Carol needed to tend to the customers in the café. I didn't want to intrude on Sarah's personal space, but I didn't have much of a choice. Once I got her into her apartment, I felt like an intruder. It felt wrong to be in there.

When I walked into her apartment, I had the weirdest sensation, though. It felt so homey. I didn't expect it to be so welcoming and cozy. I didn't dare look around; I knew if she was alert, she wouldn't want me in here. I put Sarah straight on to her bed and pulled the blanket up over her. I stared at her for a minute to make sure she was breathing okay. She scared the shit out of me when she fainted earlier. As soon as I saw her chest rise and fall and felt her heartbeat in her wrist, I booked it out of her apartment.

I went back downstairs to ask Jess or Carol if they wanted to go up and check on Sarah, but when I got back down to the café, a bus was pulling up with a full college soccer team from Rose Point. Jess and Carol looked panicked, so I offered to help them for a minute. Carol looked at me like I had grown a third head. I quickly explained that I used to work at a coffee shop in the city and could make drinks as long as they showed me where a few items were.

Jess didn't ask questions; she simply said, "Come on back!" So I grabbed an apron from the back room and stepped in. Making coffee and smiling at customers was the most fun I've had in weeks, but I was definitely exhausted when I saw the pile of work waiting at my own job later.

I miss my job at the coffee shop. I miss when things were simpler. I miss not worrying about the future or what's next.

When I got in last night, I called my brother Eric. He's my oldest younger brother. I made small talk with him, asked how things were going, and then got to the point—how much longer until he is done with his degree? I have to know because the answer directly correlates with how much longer I'm stuck doing a job I hate. How much longer until I need to know what's next.

The next day, I wake up to an email from Sarah. My heart races.

> *Hey Chaiguy87,*
>
> *I'm disappointed you don't know what TTFN is; Tigger would be incredibly disappointed. It stands for Ta-Ta For Now!*
>
> *My employee is feeling much better; however I ended up with the sickness too—looks like it was just a twenty-four-hour thing. I'm already feeling more myself.*
>
> *It was so hard, though; yesterday was the first day I had to accept outside help with my business.*
>
> *I've been sick before but can usually just work in the back, place shipments, and still help clean. Yesterday, I had to leave. I didn't even get a say in it.*
>
> *My arch enemy worked in my cafe; the one I'm trying to save because of him. I work so hard, and it was so frustrating to be forced into a break. I can't afford a break right now. I need to be my very best.*

Anyway, I do have a social media presence. It's not the best, so I'm starting there first. I reached out to some food and travel influencers; maybe one of them will come do a video on my business.

I find it fascinating that you mix up your coffee order. I'm curious—is it because it's always from a different place? Or do you switch up even from the same place?

I love a good whiskey occasionally. Maybe when we meet up soon, we can grab one? I won't lie . . . I didn't think I'd see this through to the end. I didn't think I'd actually plan to meet whoever I talked to, but it feels good talking to you. So, even if it only ends in friendship, I'm excited at the idea of meeting you in person someday soon.

Gotta get to work now that I'm feeling okay. Talk soon!

TTFN, Coffeegal13

I smile. She's excited to meet me. Then I frown, because she's not going to be happy when she finds out. I only hope I've shared enough by then that she understands me.

I glance at the clock and realize I don't have enough time to reply to Sarah before work. I'll have to answer her later this evening.

I get ready quickly and head out front. Liam is already out there leaning against his car and texting on his phone. He glances up as I walk up. "Sup you ready for some coffee?"

"Yep!" I pull my jacket against me tighter. It's windy and a bit brisk today.

"Cool. Don't bail on me for half the day again to-day—ok?" He glares at me across the car.

"Was just helping out. You saw her, man," I defend.

"Yeah, but you have your own work to do too. You need to embrace your new life. Embrace the money; embrace the power." He smirks. "You could have a damn good life if you would just embrace it, bro."

"Yeah, sure." I shrug. There is no sense in arguing with him about how much I hate it. We've done it before; he just doesn't understand.

I hop into his car and blow into my hands to warm them up.

He drives off toward Sarah's coffee shop, and my heart skips a beat.

CHAPTER TWENTY-SIX

Sarah

I AM HUMILIATED AFTER yesterday. In all my years, I've never been that sick. Luckily, just as Carol said, after sleeping fifteen hours straight, I'm feeling better. Still not 100 percent but enough that I can work in the back today and help out if Jess or Carol need it.

Even though it was a miserable twenty-four hours, I'm grateful that's all it was. I could not afford to be out for a week with the flu right now.

On the off chance another bus full of people comes by, I'll be ready.

I woke up this morning and thought Ethan helping out in the café was one of my fever dreams, but Jess explained it wasn't. To be fair, I had *a lot* of wild fever dreams yesterday. Most of which involved Ethan.

Which is incredibly frustrating. We only went on one date. Half of the date was shitty. I'm not sure why my brain can't seem to get enough of him.

He worked here half of the day yesterday. I can't believe he did that. More importantly, *why* did he do that?

Is he trying to steal my information or recipes? Jess insists he just felt bad and stepped in and offered to help. She says he's a 'good person.' I think he is up to no good, though. I appreciate his help yesterday, but it 100 percent won't be happening again. He is a jerk, and I don't know why he helped, but I don't trust it.

I opened up the café this morning, and Jess and Carol came in early for opening in case I was sick again. I'm currently in the back processing shipments of new cups and a couple of new syrups to try.

Jess peeks her head in. "Hey, Sis. Ethan and Liam just got here in case you maybe wanted to say . . . Thanks? Ya know, for yesterday?" She smiles and walks out, leaving me unable to respond.

I sigh. I don't want to say thank you. I don't trust the jerk.

The polite thing to do, though, would be to say thank you and offer him some type of compensation for the hours he worked yesterday.

I get up and honestly, my fatigue hits me in the chest like a ton of bricks. I'm still utterly exhausted despite my stomach feeling better. I get my feet under me and head out into the café.

Liam and Ethan are finishing up their order with Jess. Ethan glances over like he already knows I'm there and frowns slightly.

He strolls over and puts his hands in his pockets. "You okay today? Really scared a few of us yesterday."

I stare at him blankly for a second, because surely he wasn't the one scared . . . right?

My mind sputters for a beat, and then I say, "Uh yeah. I'm fine. Thanks for, uh, yesterday and stuff. Sorry about things. Do you, uh, want any compensation for your hours worked here? How many hours was it exactly?"

I know I'm rambling, but I can't seem to get the proper words out. After countless steamy fever dreams about this man, I'm finding it hard to form words while looking at him. All I can picture is his hand around my neck, while the other one . . . Nope. Focus, Sarah.

He smirks as though he can read all my thoughts, and I can feel my face turning bright red. I pull at the collar of my 1980s band T-shirt as though that will cool down my skin enough to stop my face from blushing.

"I don't need any *compensation,* Sarah; I was happy to help! I'm just glad you're feeling better. Although, I would still recommend taking it easy." The way he says the word compensation makes me immediately regret my word choice.

"Right, okay. Well thank you so much for helping. I don't know how I'll ever repay you. It was very . . . uh . . . thoughtful, I guess," I stutter. I don't know why he did it. Is it because he is thoughtful? That wouldn't seem right based on what I know about Ethan.

"Also, I don't need you to tell me to take it easy. How utterly manly of you to tell a woman what to do or what she feels in her body. I know what I can handle," I snap. I'm so fucking tired, and I don't need him telling me to take it easy. There's a reason I'm not out here making coffee.

"I didn't mean it like that. I was just worried, wanted you to get more rest . . . " his voice gets quieter at the end, like he realized he should've kept his dang mouth shut.

"I'm sure me getting more rest would make your business a lot easier," I mumble under my breath. "Well, whatever. I don't need your help," I insist louder.

"No problem, Sarah. I just hope you feel better soon." Keeping his hands in his pockets, he walks away. I can't help but wonder about him. He's definitely a jerk. He lied to me; he is opening a Starbucks in my town and yet continues to come here for coffee. Maybe, though, I'm missing something? He seems genuine about stepping in and helping yesterday.

He also seems to know how to make coffee. Did he work inside a Starbucks long ago? I'm not sure anymore.

I glance at Jess, who winks at me. Good lord, she knows I hate him, right? Did she even see that interaction? I snapped at him. I roll my eyes at her and head back to the office. I sit in my chair and put my head on my desk. It's pounding, probably from dehydration, but I'm going to continue to drink my coffee anyway. I need the caffeine kick.

I sigh. There is a knock on the office door. "Yep!" I yell as I lift my head up. The movement immediately makes my head spin.

"Hi, doll," Carol drawls at me. "Just checkin' on ya. You doing okay, hun?"

"Yep! All good, why? Do you guys need help out there?" I turn my chair to get up if I need to.

"Nah, we are good, love. We're slow out there now that those boys left. Just wanted to make sure you were okay. You're my bestie for the restie and all," she says as she smiles at me.

I laugh. "Carol, where did you hear that phrase?"

"Your sister, of course!" She chuckles. "She thinks it's sad I'm your bestie. Cause I'm *so* old, but little does she know I'm a hoot! I'm a riot! You know! I think you've got a great bestie because I can give age-old advice."

I smile at her, cause it's hard not to. "Advice, huh? What do I need advice on?"

Carol sits across from me, reaches over, and grabs my hand. "A few things, hun. One, life is too short to stay mad at people. Either let it go or hash it out, but it ain't worth ya troubles. Two, life is too short to ignore a man who clearly likes you. Whether it's a forever love or just a fun time, you deserve that. And three, ask for help and take it. Accept that sometimes people want to help because they love ya. It's not always for a bigger purpose." She drops my hand and walks to the door.

She turns and looks my way before heading out. "I gotta get back out there, Boss Lady, but I wanted to let you know. Ethan was a really big help yesterday. Don't read too much into it." She winks and leaves me alone with my thoughts.

I heard what she said, but I still don't trust him. Maybe it's the cynic in me.

Dear Coffeegal13,

I'm so sorry to hear you got sick. How are you feeling today? Are you better? Do you need anything? Not that I'm much help virtually, but maybe.

I know being sick totally sucks, but sometimes, our body forces us to take a break when we refuse to give it one. Maybe you have needed a break for a while? It sounds like you work a lot. Maybe the universe was trying to give you the break you deserve.

I'm also so sorry I disappointed you with my lack of knowledge on Winnie the Pooh. I made sure to google other important facts and quotes on Winnie the Pooh to not upset you further. I couldn't possibly live with more of your disappointment.

I can't wait to hear more about your social media. I'm sure someone will agree to come do a piece on your business. It sounds like an incredible business, and they would be lucky to be a part of it.

I'm not sure why I always mix up my coffee order? I wish I had a more interesting answer for you. When

I used to work in a coffee shop, I wanted to try all the drinks. That's how it started. I wanted to be able to explain flavor profiles to customers, share what different drinks tasted like. Ever since then, I mix up what I order. However, I always love a Dirty Chai. That's typically my go-to nowadays. Unless it's a new place I'm not familiar with, then I'll order an Americano because no one can screw up an Americano—unless the espresso is just downright awful, in which case I wouldn't want anything from them anyway.

Got any big plans this week? Reading any good books? I enjoy hearing about your daily life for some reason. I may sound pathetic, but I didn't realize I was lonely until I started talking to you. It's been a breath of fresh air to look forward to my email every day. I'll just be here patiently waiting for the next one!
-Chaiguy87

I stare at the screen that night, reading Chaiguy87's message over and over. Not because I think he is pathetic, but because I actually feel the same way. I stare at the screen because he said he orders Americanos and chai lattes. His explanation has me confused. I've judged so many people harshly over the years.

Hell, I judged Ethan. Who ordered an Americano, and a ... chai latte. I hate Ethan. Am I going to hate Chaiguy87 too? No, I don't think so. chaiguy is open and honest. He didn't lie to me. He already told me some vague details about his job, and he seems like he is a caring guy.

I try not to think too much about it. Chaiguy87 is different, and maybe he will end up being just a friend, and Ethan . . . well, Ethan is nothing. Just a guy I went on one date with that I happen to fantasize about a lot now.

Carol was right. I can't let Ethan bother me, especially because we were nothing. One date, and then I found out he was a liar. He's a walking red flag, and he is someone else's problem.

I reply to Chaiguy87 and let him know that my big plans for the week are reading my new romance novel and cuddling with Trixie on the couch.

The next morning, I'm up early to open the café. Everything is clean and ready when I unlock the front door and let a few of the early morning regulars in.

When I hit the first morning lull, I walk out from behind the counter to wipe down a few tables.

Ethan walks in, and I glance at the clock on the wall.

"You're early," I grumble at him.

His eyes meet mine. "Aw, Sarah, are you keeping track of my schedule?"

"Goodness no, I couldn't care less about your schedule. I just know what time you and Liam usually come in . . . " I say as I move back around the counter to take his order.

"Well, yeah, it turns out Liam caught your little twenty-four-hour stomach bug now, so I'm on my own and don't have to wait around for him . . . " He moves to the register.

We stand on either side of the register, staring at each other.

"It's quiet in here today . . . " He gestures around the empty store.

"It always is at this time. It's the calm before the storm. It's my favorite part of the day." As soon as I say the words, I want to take them back. He doesn't deserve to know my favorite anything.

"Sarah, I . . . " Ethan starts sympathetically.

"Don't. Ethan, just don't. I don't want an explanation. I don't care. You lied to me on that first date, and I'm done," I snap.

He reels back and looks as though I've personally slapped him across the face.

"What do you want to drink?" I wake up the register and get ready to press the buttons for whatever drink he orders.

"I'll do an iced brown sugar shaken espresso today . . . Please." He gives me a weak smile, and it's one I don't return.

"Sure. Great. That'll be five dollars and seventy-five cents," I respond.

He hands me seven dollars in cash. "Keep the change," he grumbles.

I look up from the register and back at this face. We just stand there and stare at each other for a long second. For a brief minute, I *wish* I was in the habit of giving second chances.

This business is mine, and it's all I have. I'd do anything to keep it successful. I don't know why he lied to me, but I don't care. I need to protect this business at all costs, because without it, I have nothing.

I finally look away from his stupid gorgeous eyes and begin to make his drink. Shaken espresso happens to be one of my favorites to make.

I wouldn't ever admit that to him, though.

When I finish up, I turn to hand it to him. He's staring at me from behind the counter. Eyes dark, watching with rapt attention. I hand his cup over, and our hands brush.

"Have a great day, Sarah . . . " he says in a soft, firm voice. That tone sends a jolt of heat down my spine. It's a voice meant for audiobook narration, if I'm being perfectly honest.

I stand there staring at the door he just walked out of, at war with myself for a good minute.

Carol walks in through the door. "You good, Boss Lady? You sick again?" she says as she walks in.

"No, Carol, I'm fine. Just tired . . . " I lie.

CHAPTER
TWENTY-SEVEN

Ethan

THE NEXT COUPLE OF weeks pass in the blink of an eye. Every day is the same. Liam and I go to Daisy Ridge Coffee Co. I happen to believe Liam is very addicted to their coffee. Not sure what he will do when we leave Daisy Ridge, honestly. After grabbing coffee, we head to the job site. Construction is going well, and I have mixed feelings about that because I feel guilty. I feel responsible for Sarah's business for some reason.

I know it's not my problem, but I'm only human. I feel like we are ruining a beautiful and talented girl's life.

When Liam and I finish work, he heads off to whatever flavor of the week's bed. I think it might be Jess again? Or maybe it's Trish? I can't keep up.

I head to my room alone. Some nights, I watch Law and Order, other nights, I read the fantasy book Sarah said she likes, but every night, I message with my Coffeegal13.

It's starting to feel weird that I know it's Sarah but she doesn't know it's me. I'm starting to think the plan will backfire. I make sure I repeatedly mention how I hate my job. I tell her I hope my younger brother can take my spot sooner rather than later. I tell her I just want to do something that makes me happy.

At the end of the day, I hope when she finds out it's me, she understands. If she's mad, I can handle that, as long as she at least understands. I don't *want* to be ruining her life.

We are officially one week out from our Rose Point Books Meet up where we will find out just how pissed Sarah actually is. That's when Jess tells Liam and me that Carnation Springs does a Singles' Night once a year and tells us we should come.

When I say absolutely not, she says, "Well, it's tomorrow night, and Sarah will be there." And then she winks at me.

My stomach does a pancake flip. The rational part of my brain knows exactly why Sarah is going to a singles' night. The irrational part is wondering if Sarah isn't happy chatting with Chaiguy87. Why is she going to a singles' night when she's so close to meeting him . . . I mean, me?

It takes my brain a minute to compute. Then I tell Jess, "Great! Sarah deserves to find someone and be happy here." She gives me a side-eye. She sighs and shrugs.

She starts to walk away and calls over her shoulder, "I'll text you the details."

We're going to Singles' Night. After a lot of protest, Liam and Jess convinced me that we all needed to go. Liam and Jess both want to find someone, and Liam threw a toddler-sized tantrum about needing a wingman. So, here I am heading for Carnation Springs on a Friday night. I took the top off my Jeep, and told Liam I'd drive separately. I did it mostly for myself, but also so he could end up in whatever bed he wants, and I don't have to worry about the big dumb idiot.

I've never been to Carnation Springs, so I drive up a bit early. The event doesn't start until 7, but I'm enjoying cruising around the town with the wind in my hair. I'm comfortable for the first time in weeks wearing my Converse, riding in my Jeep, with my maroon henley tee on. I tap the steering wheel as I sing along to "There She Goes" by Sixpence None the Richer. I drive down the town's main street, and I can't help but smile. It's cute. It's lined with street lights all sporting pink and red Singles' Night flags and signs. String lights bounce back and forth across the paved street.

Every shop is a brick two-story with various colored canopies. Some have signs out front urging people in; others have tables and chairs. The street is lined with trees, plants, and flowers of every color. It's only a few blocks, but it's . . . well, it's something that makes you instantly want to walk up and down holding someone's hand.

My mom would love it. I find a parking spot and decide I should find a little knick-knack for her with the town name on it. It'll remind me to tell her about this place, and maybe we can make a trip someday. I don't think she's up for a trip quite yet, not without Dad, but hopefully someday soon.

In the meantime, I'll find her something nice. Maybe a magnet for her fridge. I hop out of the car and start walking up the street. Everyone is smiling and relaxed. It seems like Singles' Night draws a crowd, as there are a lot of girls walking up and down in groups with friends. I walk up to a shop with a sign that reads, Carnation Gifts & More. It sounds promising for something for my mom.

I walked around for a while, enjoying feeling comfortable and somewhat relaxed for the first time in a while. I immediately get hit with a pang of guilt. I shouldn't be happy yet; I should be grieving. I should miss my dad.

I grab Mom a magnet that has the *Welcome to Carnation Springs* sign on it and pay. As I walk out of the shop, I notice Sarah's yellow car out of the corner of my eye. It's parked in front of Carnation Springs Café and Carnation Music Shop. I start walking in that direction without even thinking. I pass the music shop and glance through the window. There are instruments and sheet music on one side and vinyl records on the other. I don't see Sarah and keep walking. When I get to Carnation Springs Café, I see Sarah through the window sitting at the bar. I walk in, and the chime on the door rings. Sarah looks my way and immediately rolls her eyes.

Carnation Springs Café looks like a 1950s diner inside. The bar top is a sparkly white with rounded edges. The stools are red and silver, and Sarah looks absolutely gorgeous sitting there drinking a beverage with a straw twisted and shaped like a heart. She has jeans on, an oversized Rolling Stones graphic tee, and her hair is down in a mess of waves. Of course, she is rocking her Converse. I glance down at my own, now feeling very self-conscious.

I walk up to the bar top, and Sarah glances at me again. "Mind if I sit here?" I gesture to the stool next to hers.

"Yeah, whatever," she grumbles at me.

I take a seat next to her, and a young lady behind the counter brings me a menu and asks if I'd like anything to drink.

"Do you have coffee?" I ask.

"Oh yes, we just have a pot, though, nothing fancy," she answers.

"Great, I'll take a black coffee with cream, please," I say with a smile.

She smiles back and winks at me, "Be back in a sec!"

I turn to Sarah, whose face is twisted in a grimace.

"Yuck, it was hard to watch that poor girl fawn over you." She shakes her head and returns to sipping whatever drink is in front of her.

"Careful, Sarah, you sound jealous." I smile at her.

She turns away from me again, mumbling, "Absolutely not." She adds a gagging noise at the end, and I chuckle.

The waitress brings over my coffee, and I thank her. She walks away, taking another customer's drink order.

I take a sip, turn to Sarah, and say, "It's not as good as yours."

Sarah sighs. "What are you doing, Ethan? I'm not in the mood."

I frown. "What am I doing here? Or what am I doing with this coffee? I'm here because Liam and Jess told me I needed to come here for some silly Singles' Night. I've never been to Carnation Springs so I came a bit early to check it out. Why are you here?"

"I'm here because every year, Carol forces me to close early and tells me to come to Carnation Springs for Singles' Night. My mom loved it, and Carol knows that. She thinks it's important I come 'for my mom.' Plus, no one is really getting coffee in Daisy Ridge while this event happens anyway." She sighs. "I came to see my old friends at Carnation Springs Coffee, but it seems they've closed down in the past year. Probably some jack-ass opening a Starbucks or something." She glares at me.

"Well it wasn't me. I'm very sorry to hear your friends had to close up shop. That must've been hard for them. Maybe you can open a second location here in Carnation Springs? Your café is incredible. I bet it would do well here." I sip my coffee. "They could use some good coffee in this town, too."

"Well isn't that just like *you*, telling me to take over someone's business after they've barely left. The coffee is probably still warm, ya know? Do you think about anything other than yourself and business, Mr. Hot Shot?" She pulls her sparkly pink heart-shaped purse up off the chair and rummages through it. She throws a ten-dollar bill down. "I guess I'll see you tonight, *Mr. Americano.*" She hops off the chair and blows right out the door.

I won't lie. I don't even care. She's pissing me off with her judgy attitude.

CHAPTER TWENTY-EIGHT

Sarah

AFTER STORMING OUT ON Ethan in Carnation Springs Café, I stroll up and down Main Street, looking in all the shops. This is the one evening I take for myself each year. I only close early twice a year, for Singles' Night in Carnation Springs and for the Christmas Festival in Daisy Ridge Park.

Maybe someday, it'll only be once a year. Maybe someday, I won't be single and forced to take this time off. Maybe I'll end up with Chaiguy87.

Although, Mom loved Singles' Night in Carnation Springs. She would always come, even though she was fully in love with Dad in every way.

She always said Singles' Night for Carnation Springs was the only way all the shops here stayed in business. Most people make a weekend out of coming here with their friends. There are a few bed-and-breakfasts nearby and little cabin rentals down by the Springs. It is a nice place for a weekend getaway.

Maybe someday, I'll hire another employee and do a weekend away here. Right now, it seems pointless because coming alone feels pathetic.

I know it shouldn't, but it does. I feel a twinge of loneliness in my chest. I don't have friends like Jess does. I never really have. I have my business, Jess, and Carol. That's always been enough for me.

Sometimes, though, I get jealous of Jess. Her ability to travel around and do fun things with her friends. I just don't have that, and I'm not sure I ever will.

Talking to Chaiguy87 feels good, though. I actually have been opening up a lot the past couple of weeks. It feels easy since I don't know him. I might be naïve. He could be a total creep, but for now, it's nice to just tell someone everything.

I love Jess, Carol, and my dad, but I can't tell them *everything*. Especially Dad, he would worry. I don't want that.

I check out every shop in Carnation Springs. I buy a few little things from some of them. I know Mom would want me to support them, and I can't help but feel like I should since Carnation Coffee closed. Carnation Coffee is where I got my start; it's where I learned everything I know.

I did think about what Ethan said, though. There was a moment earlier when the thought passed through my head. I considered a second location here—it's close enough to commute but far enough away that there isn't direct competition.

The old Carnation Coffee storefront is available. There is a sign up in the window. I took a picture of the phone number listed but immediately felt guilty about it.

Then Ethan said it, and I knew I should feel guilty because he is an ass, and what the hell, I don't want to think like that man. I still don't know why the hell he had the nerve to sit next to me.

I head to meet Jess before the official Singles' Night Speed Dating.

Singles' Night goes like this—speed dating, cocktail hour, and then date night or, as I call it, freedom. You are supposed to try to pick a date by the *freedom* part and go out afterward, but that's usually when I leave and head back to Daisy Ridge.

Jess is standing outside of Carnation Cocktails, which is a little dive bar at the end of Main Street. They host the speed dating and cocktail hour, and I'm pretty sure it's dead the rest of the year.

Jess is wearing a silver form-fitting dress with her signature black leather jacket on top. She has black tights and black heel booties on. Her hair is gorgeously curled, and her lips are painted red, as usual.

She's a smoke show. She's stunning. I don't have it in me to care about my appearance nearly as much as her. When she looks up from her phone and sees me, she frowns.

"Sarah, good god. Why don't you at least try to get ready for a date for once? You'd probably have every guy in here if you would just dress up!" she shouts at me.

"Hi, Jess. Nice to see you too! I know, I *am* the best sister for coming here and doing this with you year after year, even though I don't want to." I smile at her. This event is my least favorite thing ever, but I'll do anything for Jess, and I know my mom would want me to do this.

She grumbles, "Ugh, whatever, Sarah. Let's gooooo! I'm ready to meet the love of my life."

I want to tell her that she probably won't meet the love of her life at a speed dating event, but I suppose it isn't going to help either of us if I say it out loud.

We head inside, and it is packed, probably even busier than last year if that's even possible.

Jess starts waving at someone across the room. My eyes move to see who—Liam and Ethan. "Why are you waving at them? I thought you and Liam broke up?" I whisper to her.

Jess looks my way. "Yeah, we did, but we are still *friends* if you know what I mean." She wiggles her eyebrows and winks.

"Ew. No. Nope. I don't know what you mean, and I don't want to. Gross." I turn and look around the room. Every table has a number on it. There are people lining the bar and already grabbing drinks.

I make my way to the bar and wait a few minutes.

Ethan comes up on my left, brushing my shoulder, and I wish he wasn't so damn attractive. It would make hating his guts much easier.

Ethan turns and says, "Can I get your drink? Vodka tonic?"

"And why would you do that? So you could poison it?" I turn to look at him.

The bar is so full, that we are practically pressed against each other. His jaw is flexed, and his eyes are dark. He looks like he might slap me across the face with his heated stare, and for some reason, heat rushes down my spine at the thought. Maybe I've been reading too many dark romance books lately.

Ethan straightens and stands taller. "No, Sarah, it's just because I like you. As much as you want to make me a villain, I'm just a nice guy. But I'm kind of over this whole thing where you paint me as evil and don't let me defend myself. Storming out before I can get a word in. Do you want a free drink or not?" He stares into my eyes.

Ethan is handsome. Obviously, I've fantasized about him enough to know I find him attractive. Right now, though, he just told me how it is, and it was hot . . . Is he a jerk? Or am I completely turned on?

"Uh, yeah, okay," I mumble. "Vodka tonic."

He turns and gets the bartender's attention and orders our drinks. He orders a whiskey neat. When she brings the drinks back, he pays and hands me my drink. "See you during the speed dating, Sarah." And he turns and heads off. I watch his retreating back disappear into the crowd.

Jess comes up and grabs me by the arm. "Come on, silly. It's time to staaaart!" She has a grin so wide, it seems like her cheeks are about to burst.

Speed dating is a complete disaster.

The event is too big this year, so they split everyone up and take some people next door to Carnation Springs Grocery as overflow. Ethan and Liam are in the group that goes there, so I don't even see them through speed dating.

I talk to about fifty guys, a minute and a half per guy. They changed it from the three minutes each they did last year because of the number of people. It's crazy, and I wish I hadn't come. I hate crowds, and I'm so uncomfortable. A minute and a half is not nearly enough time for a conversation either.

All fifty guys I talk to aren't from around here. Which is great for Carnation Springs, I suppose, but not super great for a relationship with me. I'm even farther out of town, so Carnation Springs is about as long distance as I'm willing to try.

Some of the guys are nice enough, but there is no spark. Some of the guys are total douche canoes.

Some of the guys are incredibly nerdy, not that there's anything wrong with being a nerd, but if they are a nerd who is still playing video games in their mom's basement, it's a no for me, dawg.

I don't have all my shit together, but I'm young and own a business. I don't need a man-child who lives with his momma.

During cocktail hour, they let everyone back into Carnation Cocktails. A few guys who are in the other group come up and introduce themselves. Two offer to buy me a drink, but I decline. I want to drive home tonight, so one drink two hours ago is enough for me. I look around the room for Jess, but my eyes instantly find Ethan instead.

He's trying to ruin my business, right? There is absolutely nothing he could say to make me like him. He said earlier I haven't given him a chance, but I did. I gave him the perfect opportunity at Delano's, and he skirted around the question, instead of telling me whatever he thinks I need to know.

His eyes find mine, and we just stare at each other across the room for a minute. I give him a small smile, and he smiles back but continues talking to the girl in front of him. His eyes stay on mine for another second before I break away to look for Jess again. I find her in the corner with not one, not two, but three guys talking to her. Luckily, Liam isn't one of them, so I don't have to punch a bro. At least not yet.

I start making my way through the crowd to Jess, when the announcer comes on the mic and says it's time for date night. I have to book it out of here before some jerkoff comes and asks me out tonight.

I get to Jess, and she smiles and yells, "Sarah!!!" She wraps me in a hug. She lets me go and looks into my eyes. "You're leaving, aren't you?" She pouts, giving me her very best sad puppy dog face.

I laugh. "Yeah, hun. I'm leaving, gotta wake up early! I'll see you tomorrow, though. Call me if you need anything and be safe!" I glare at her.

"Yeah, okay, I'll be suuuuuuper safe." She winks at me and then blows a kiss. "Thanks for coming, Sis. Love you."

"Love you too, little brat!" I run my hand down her arm and give her hand a squeeze.

I make my way out of the bar, working hard to not make eye contact with a single person, as everyone starts pairing up and heading out.

I get outside and rub my arms against the cool breeze. There is a chill in the air that wasn't there earlier when the sun was out.

I start walking quickly to my car, trying to get there as fast as I can so I can warm up a bit. After a few minutes, I see my yellow beauty and climb in. I blow on my hands and rub them together. I get my keys out of my purse and start the car . . . Except it doesn't start. I try again, and nothing happens. *Shit.*

CHAPTER TWENTY-NINE

Ethan

I MADE IT OUT of Singles' Night in one piece. I won't lie, the girls here were pushy. It was hard to get out without feeling bad. I know more than one was hoping I'd ask them out tonight. It seemed like most girls ended up with a date, though, or better yet, ended up with a group of girlfriends heading for what everyone was referring to as "the better bar."

I'm in my Jeep and deeply regretting taking the top off earlier. It was so nice out before, but now there's a cold bite to the air and the clouds are rolling in. I'm just really hoping I can make it back to Daisy Ridge without it raining.

As I drive down Main Street, I see Sarah's yellow car. I feel a pang of sadness at the idea of her being out with another man, but as I get closer, I notice the hood is up. It looks like she's rummaging around under there.

I quickly pull into a spot next to her.

"You okay?" I shout as I get out of my car.

She looks up, and she's got grease up to her elbows and even some on her forehead.

"Uh, yeah, I'm okay. Go back to your date or whatever. I'm pretty sure it's just the battery." She turns her face back down into the hood. I walk around and come up next to her.

"I'm not a car guy, but I can try to give you a jump? I've got cables." I look down into her car. It's old, and it doesn't look like she takes the best care of it.

I run over and grab the cables, and we try jumping a few times with no success. After about five minutes of helping her and trying a few different things, I realize she has to be freezing. I run to my passenger door, swing it open, and grab my sweater for her. I come around and hand it to her.

"What's this for?" She glares at me while her teeth chatter, and her body shivers.

"For warmth. Don't argue, just put it on," I snip as I turn and keep trying to get her car to start. She reluctantly puts it on, rubs her arms, and puts her hands in the pockets.

She doesn't say thanks, but she wouldn't be the Sarah I've come to enjoy if she did. I keep tinkering with her car and ask "Is there a shop nearby?"

"Uhm, Carnation Springs has some kind of auto shop, I think? Not sure what it's called or where it is." She pulls out her phone and starts typing.

I put the hood down. "Listen, I can keep messing with it, but I think our best bet would be to have someone come get it, and I'll take you home."

She scrunches her face as she thinks.

"Ok," she says.

"Ok? You don't want to argue with me about it first?" I smile at her.

"No." She glares at me. "I need this car taken care of *properly,* and I need to get home. It's late, and I have an early morning."

"Okay. I'll find a tow truck to call." I pull out my phone and find the number for the nearest auto shop.

A nice guy named Thomas answers and tells me he's the "after hours on call guy" and he'd be happy to come grab "old yeller" after I explained to him the car was yellow.

Sarah and I wait in absolute silence for twelve minutes until Thomas gets there. She gives him her keys, and he lets her know they will call in the morning with an update.

I tell him thank you and shake his hand. I go over and open the passenger door of my Jeep for Sarah, and she climbs in.

I walk around and get in to start the car.

I notice Sarah is staring at me, almost as if she is confused and wants to say something but doesn't quite know what.

I start heading back toward Daisy Ridge. It's late and quiet, and the music on the radio is just a low hum as we head down Route 88. It's definitely cold with the top off, but when I look over at Sarah, she looks happy. Her hand is out the window going up and down in the breeze. A small smile rests on her lips as she looks out the window, and it makes me smile in return.

It's peaceful, just like it was the last time we rode in the car together. It's silent, but not uncomfortable.

We reach a stoplight, and Sarah glances over at me and says, "Thank you. I appreciate the ride home."

"No problem." I grip the steering wheel to keep myself from reaching for her hand.

Suddenly, I feel a drop of water on my hand, and I glance up at the sky. The dark clouds are directly above us, and it starts to sprinkle.

The light turns green, and I step on the gas. We are only about six minutes away from Sarah's, and I'm determined to get her there as dry as possible. It starts raining even harder, and I look over as Sarah starts laughing.

Her makeup starts running down her face, her hair is frizzing, and she looks radiant. She looks carefree and happy. It's the most relaxed I've ever seen her, and it's a gorgeous sight.

She leans her head back against the seat and looks up at the sky smiling.

I make it to her place, pull into the tiniest covering, and turn the Jeep off. My Jeep is only half covered, but I quickly get out of the car and walk around to open Sarah's door. She's still smiling, and I reach for her hand to help her out. She reluctantly takes my hand and swings her legs around. When her feet are firmly on the ground, I'm still holding her hand.

She looks up at me, makeup streaks down her face in the pouring rain. She pulls my hand and says, "Come on, let's at least get you dry before you head home. It's the least I can do for your help." She lets go of my hand, and I instantly miss the warmth.

I carefully follow her up the slippery wet stairs, and I immediately want to make them safer for her, add runners to them or something. This is definitely a hazard when it rains.

Just as that thought passes my mind, she starts to slip when there are only three steps left, and I catch her and help her back up. "Sorry, thanks," she mumbles.

The rain starts to pick up, pouring down on us both. I don't know what I'm going to do about the Jeep. I know it'll be fine. It's built for this, but the seats will definitely stink for a little while.

Sarah leads me into her apartment, and I instantly shiver at the change in temperature as I close the door behind me. I hear a meow from the other room, and Trixie comes bounding toward us. She immediately goes to Sarah, who reaches down and pets her. "Hi, baby girl. Did you miss me?" she says as she pets her.

Trixie then comes for me, and she starts to weave in between my legs. I bend down and scratch behind her ear, and she immediately begins to purr.

I look up at Sarah, who is staring at me like I just grew horns. "You ok?" I ask.

"Uh, yeah, Trixie just doesn't usually like men." She turns away. "Let me grab you a towel. I might have a shirt big enough for you too, but I don't have pants." She chuckles as she walks into her room.

She comes back out a minute later with two plush purple towels and a Van Halen T-shirt that is my size.

"Do I want to know where this shirt came from?" I raise my eyebrow at her as I grab the shirt and towel from her.

She laughs. "It's just mine. I buy big T-shirts to sleep in, and sometimes, I even wear them to work." She starts drying her hair with the other towel. Squeezing all the water out.

"Are you calling me big?" I chuckle.

She snorts. "God, no! You just have like . . . muscles?"

"Why, Sarah, have you been admiring my muscles?" I smirk at her.

"Ugh, no! You're just . . . You know!" she stammers.

We both laugh.

Trixie starts dancing around the kitchen counter meowing, and there is an awkward silence while Sarah and I stare at each other.

Sarah jumps a little. "Oh shoot. Sorry, Trix, you must be hungry." She sets the towel down on one of the two barstools at her kitchen counter and feeds Trixie. She puts her bowl directly on the counter. I'm sure most people would find that weird, but why should Sarah? It's just her and Trixie up here, and by the looks of it, this place is just as much Trixie's as it is Sarah's.

I pull my shirt over my head. Sarah is rinsing Trixie's water bowl in the sink with her back toward me. "Hey, Do you have somewhere I can dry my wet shirt off?" I ask.

"Oh yeah, there is a laundry room right there where that door is." She turns to point to the door behind me and drops the water bowl when she looks at me.

"Shit," she murmurs.

"Oh, I can help!" I drop my wet shirt on the table for a second and grab one of the towels to start drying my bare chest.

"Oh, uh, no, I'm good. Just, uh, put that wet shirt in the laundry room quickly please," she says, completely avoiding eye contact with me.

I get up and move to grab my wet shirt, thinking maybe the table I set it on is special. Maybe she wants it off the table as fast as possible to not ruin it.

I grab the shirt and make my way over to the laundry room.

CHAPTER THIRTY

Sarah

Ethan is here.

He is in my apartment.

He is shirtless.

I've had too many dreams about him lately to deny my attraction, but with his shirt off and his muscles flexing in front of me while he pets Trixie—I'm ready to jump him in my living room.

You know those firefighter calendars where some jacked dude is holding a kitten in nothing but suspenders? That's the vibe in my living room right now. I cleaned up the water I spilled and ran to my bedroom to change and wash my face before having to face him again. When I came out, Ethan was casually carrying around Trixie as he walked along my bookshelves looking at all my spicy romance novels.

I know they are the spicy romance books because those are the only ones I keep up here in my apartment now, the rest are downstairs in the café.

Trixie meows and purrs loudly in his arms, and I can't help but wonder, why didn't he put on the fucking shirt I gave him? Why is he walking around here looking like some kind of Greek god? It's obnoxious when I've been actively trying to rewire my brain not to think about him.

I stand awkwardly in the doorway not sure what to do or where to move. I glance out the only window in my small living room, the rain looks like it has slowed down to a small drizzle. "Looks like it stopped raining . . . " My voice trails off, unsure of where I was even going with that.

Ethan glances out the window, still holding Trixie with one hand and petting her with the other as she purrs. "Oh yeah, looks like it. Well, I guess I can get out of your hair." He sets Trixie down on the floor and moves into my compact kitchen to wash his hands.

I'm staring at Trixie as if she might be able to relay her thoughts on the situation to me and maybe even provide me with some kind of advice. Of course, she can't, though. She stretches and then bounces off to hide underneath my futon couch.

I move over to my bookshelves to see where Ethan's eyes may have gone and how embarrassed I should be.

He comes up next to me. "Sorry, I didn't want to risk ruining your shirt. I just threw mine in the dryer; should be done in a second, and then I'll get out of your way. I know you have an early day tomorrow." He turns his body so his back is facing the bookshelves, his head turned toward me and his eyes on mine. I'm having a hard time remembering why it is I hate him when he is looking at me like that.

His eyes are dark as we stand there for what feels like an eternity. I step in front of him, closer than necessary, and I tell myself it's because I'm still slightly cold. His body puts off a large amount of body heat, right? Right. I'm just keeping us warm. I still hate him. This is totally normal.

He reaches for my arm and rubs the sleeve of my pajama shirt, as if he can sense I'm just trying to warm up.

His eyes move to my lips as heat makes its way down my spine. I shiver against his touch.

"Sarah . . . I . . . " He looks from my lips to my eyes. "I'm sorry, tell me to stop," he whispers.

I take another step closer and press up onto my tiptoes. Our lips are so close that I can feel his warm breath against mine.

"Fuck it," I whisper against his lips. I push him back into the bookcase and press my mouth to his.

The moment our lips touch, I immediately regret it, because no kiss will ever compare to this. *I'm ruined* is the last thought I have before he grabs my hair and my mind goes completely blank.

He spins me around, hands still in my hair, and presses me into the bookcase as he takes his time exploring me with deliciously slow kisses. His lips are demanding yet soft. He tugs at the hair along my scalp, gently pulling my head back so he can deepen the kiss. His other hand moves down my neck and rests there for a second before going down to my hip where he pulls me closer to him. It sends an instant need down my body that settles in between my thighs.

He sucks my bottom lip between his teeth, gives a small bite. I grab on to him with both my hands on his biceps and pull his body even closer. I move my one leg up slightly to give myself the tiniest bit of friction with his thigh between my legs. He moves his hand down to behind my knee and pulls my leg up around him. I let out a whimper, and I've never felt like I *needed* someone more. It's an unbearable ache I've never felt before, with my head chanting more, more, *more*.

His hand pulling my leg up gives me just the amount of friction I need to bring a tingling sensation down the length of my body. My toes curl at just that tiniest bit of pressure on me. He groans into my mouth and pulls back for a second to say, "Fuck, Sarah."

We kiss again and again. Each kiss is slower than the last. Both of us finding what the other person responds to and savoring it more.

I honestly can't process a thought other than I need more clothes off. I need more friction, I need more *him*.

A blaring alarm sounds on my phone, and at first, I think it's a fire alarm and push him off me abruptly. I stare at him wide-eyed with swollen lips. My heart moves to a gallop, as I'm trying to process what the fuck is actually happening right now.

I run around him to the kitchen where my phone is on the counter. I pick it up and glance at the screen.

"It's the café," I whisper to no one really but myself.

I run to the side of the fridge, grab my trusty baseball bat, and hurl the front door open.

"Sarah, wait!" Ethan is yelling.

I can't think.

Why did I kiss him? I hate him. Right? Yeah, I definitely hate him.

I'm down the stairs so fast and run around the corner with my bat, when I come face-to-face with Jess fumbling with keys at the front door, giggling with some guy grabbing her from behind.

"Jess! What the fuck!" I yell.

"Oh shit, sorry." She giggles and then hiccups. I immediately know she is *sooooo* drunk. "I just wanted some coffee, you know, to keep me upppppp! I'm feeling a tad sleepy, ya know?"

"Jess, give me your key." I hold out my palm face up.

"What? No! Sarah! It's fiiiiine!" she cries.

"Jess, this isn't okay. This is my life." I point at the door. "The alarm scared the shit out of me. You can have the key back when you're more responsible. It was for emergencies *only*."

Her bottom lip trembles. She looks behind me and then back at me. "Well at least you weren't scared *alone* for once." She winks at Ethan.

I know he's behind me now. I know she's winking at him. It makes me sick.

"Key, please, Jess. Now." My hand is still out in front of me waiting.

She puts the key in my hand. "For the record, I'm very upset with youuu," she slurs at me.

"Ditto," I say back.

She turns. "Can you just take me to my place?" she asks the guy who is still grabbing at her like she's the last slice of pie on Thanksgiving.

"Sure." He smiles at her and kisses her neck.

"Jess, do you want this?" I gesture to him. "You're intoxicated. I think you should have me take you home . . . " I'm trying to be as kind as possible, but this guy looks like a creep, and I'm not having it.

"I'm a big girl, Sarah! Not some freaking *child*!" she yells at me.

"I'm sorry, I just . . . " I start, but I'm interrupted by Jess barfing all over the sidewalk in front of the café.

"EW!" the creepy guy steps back yelling. "I'm outta here, babe. Call me when you're back to normal or whatever." And he takes off.

I grab Jess to hold her up. I pull her hair back with my hand, as she barfs again. "You're okay, hun." I rub her arm with the hand holding her up.

I look up and make eye contact with Ethan, and he's wearing the shirt I gave him. I guess it was probably easier to grab that than go all the way to the laundry room for his. "Can you help me get her to my apartment?" I gesture with my head to her other arm.

"Yep! On it." He comes up and grabs her other side as we carefully make our way around back to the stairs.

"I'm fine! Seriously! I'll go home!" Jess cries.

"It's fine, Jess. We will have a slumber party tonight, and you can rest at my place." I smile at her to try to ease her worry and resistance.

She looks up at me with sad eyes. Her mascara is running down her cheeks as she starts to cry. "You're always helping me," she sniffles. "I ruined your night." She reaches to wipe at her nose as we help her up the stairs.

"You've never ruined anything ever, and you couldn't if you tried." I give her a sad smile. We get her up the stairs, and we stop at my doorway. I ask Jess if she's good and tell her to go use my shower and wash up. I let her know I'll be in with a towel in a second.

She looks at Ethan and then to me. "Sorry," she whispers.

His lips tilt up with a small weak smile. "Nothing to be sorry for. Go get some rest," he whispers back.

She turns and heads toward my bathroom. I look back at Ethan. "I'm . . . " I don't even know what to say to him.

"It's fine, Sarah. Go be with Jess and try to get some rest. I'll see you tomorrow." He looks at my lips, and I can't help but think that fifteen minutes ago I was ready to get naked on the floor with this man.

I'm looking at his lips, thinking about it all, and he smiles, as if he knows exactly what I'm thinking. He turns, walks back down the stairs, and I watch his back the whole way down.

"Don't you dare dream about me tonight. I still hate you!" I yell after him, but I don't know why. The words are dead and sound like I'm trying to convince myself more than him.

He reaches the bottom step and turns to look up at me. "Having you in my dreams is better than not having you at all," he almost whispers. He says it almost like he didn't want me to hear. "Goodnight, Sarah."

CHAPTER THIRTY-ONE

Ethan

I TOSS AND TURN most of the night. I know Sarah was joking when she said not to dream of her, but I'm scared that when I do fall asleep—I'll only dream of that kiss.

It was just a kiss, and yet I don't think I can go back to life as I knew it before. How am I supposed to ever date another person again? I don't think I can. Nothing will live up to it. While that thought should terrify me, it doesn't. There has been this indescribable pull toward Sarah since the moment I met her. It's the whole reason Jess and I set up the silly charade of a messaging system.

Shit, the messaging.

I leap from the bed and pad across the room to my laptop. I flip it open, and sure enough, there is a message there from Sarah. Sadly, it's only from about an hour ago, which means she isn't getting much sleep tonight either.

Dear Chaiguy87,

I know we haven't met, and I should have no reason to feel guilty. Oddly enough, though, I do. I kissed someone tonight. Actually, I kissed my arch-enemy.

I felt like I needed to admit this to you. If I'm being honest, I just needed to admit it to someone, and you are the only one I'm truly talking to these days.

My sister and I had a bit of a disagreement earlier. We will make up in the morning, I'm sure. We've never fought for more than a few hours. I'd do anything for her, and as crazy as she can get, she knows I'll always help her.

Anyway, I don't even know what I'm saying. I'm so tired, but I couldn't sleep, so I decided to come on here. I felt the urge to let you know now that I kissed someone else tonight. On the off chance that we actually meet in six days, and really hit it off, well . . . I wanted to be truthful.

I'm rambling and should sleep. I'll send you a message tomorrow.

TTFN, Coffeegal13

I read it over and over. I feel immediate guilt. For me, she's been the same person on screen and off-screen. I've been slowly liking her more and more because she is always the same person for me.

I feel terrible that I've screwed this up again. I thought I was doing the right thing. I can't reply to this.

Up until now, I've avoided most discussion around her "arch-enemy" knowing it was me and I would have to lie outright.

I can't avoid it, though, and I can't have her continuing to feel guilty. It's just . . . Not okay.

It may be three in the morning, but I send her a message anyway.

Coffeegal13,
Never ever feel guilty for being you.
Any chance you want to break the rules and meet me a little sooner?
XO, Chaiguy87

I press send.

I don't know what comes next, but I know I'm not happy with continuing life the way it is. I want to be happy, and I'm happiest when I'm with Sarah.

CHAPTER THIRTY-TWO

Sarah

I'M DOWN IN THE café the morning after the debacle.

I came down extra early to clean Jess's *mess* off the sidewalk out front, but it was already cleaned up.

If I had to guess, I would put money on Ethan cleaning it up before he left last night, which I have mixed feelings about. I open up the café, and Carol comes in at her normal time of eight.

I got an incredibly small amount of sleep last night. I was up late worried about Jess. Once I finally got myself into bed, I began tossing and turning over the fact that I *kissed* Ethan.

It's just a kiss, but it has my knees wobbling just thinking about it and how much further it could've gone if Jess hadn't interrupted. In a way, I'm slightly thankful for Jess's interruption.

Around 9:30, there is a lull in the café, so I make Jess her iced tea and run it upstairs. She's still passed out on the bed where I left her. I gently rub her shoulder, and she opens her eyes, groaning loudly. She rubs her face as she rolls onto her back.

"Oh, Sarah, I'm so fucking sorry," she wails, covering her face with her hands.

"It's fine, Jess. You're still young. You're allowed to get drunk once in a while and make terrible decisions, as long as you learn from it and move on. Just please promise you won't be that stupid again. I don't know what would've happened if you didn't come here," I tell her.

"Honestly right now, I don't even want to *drink* ever again." She sighs. "Oooooh, is that my tea?!" She smiles at me as she sits up. "I love you so much, you know?"

I laugh. "Yeah, Sis, I know." I hand her the tea, and she takes a small sip.

"Need to pace myself, or I might puke again," she whispers.

I chuckle. "You're good, babe. I gotta go back downstairs. Clean up or sleep more. Do whatever you need. You're welcome to stay here all day if you'd like." I get up to leave.

"Wait!" Jess yells.

She startles me. I turn around, and her eyes are all glassy. "What's wrong?"

"I'm moving to Rose Point in three months . . . " she whispers.

"What?" I come back and sit down at the end of the bed.

"I'm moving to Rose Point. I got a job at a flower shop. I have three months because that's when I finish my floral design class . . . I'm excited, Sarah, but I'm scared to leave you . . . " She sniffles and wipes at her nose with the back of her hand.

"Aw, hey, this will be great. This is what you've always wanted. Rose Point isn't that far, it's only what, about two hours? You'll still be stuck seeing me at least once a week for dinner with Dad." I reach over and squeeze her other hand and smile at her. "I really gotta get back down there. We will talk more about this later, but I'm *so* proud of you, Jess. Mom would be too. Have you told Dad yet?"

"No, not yet. I'll go tell him soon, I just . . . I wanted to tell you first." She gives me a hand squeeze in return.

"Okay, well, we can even do it together if you want. I'm sorry. I gotta go. I love you, Sis." I rush out the door, and while I'm walking down the stairs, a tear falls from my eye. I held it together in front of Jess, but I'm not sure what I'll do without her. I wipe the tear away and take a deep breath as I round the corner.

I've got to keep it together until the end of the workday.

I get to the front and see Liam's stupid car out front. The guy is a total douchebag, and not just because he was stupid to Jess. It's also not because he's opening a Starbucks and comes to my café every day. He just screams douche.

I walk in, and immediately, Liam yells, "Sarah, Sarah! There she is! How ya doing, beautiful?"

He gives me what I refer to as a *cheater hug*.

You know that type of hug that's too intimate for your relationship? The squeeze with a small caress? The guy who gives every woman he meets the same hug? I don't know, maybe it's just me.

I shrug him off as I scan the café.

"I'm fine, Liam. Where's Ethan this morning? Not that I'm looking for him, of course. You guys just usually come in together . . . "

Liam laughs. "Yeah, of course, you wouldn't be looking for Ethan. You *hate* him."

I can't tell if he is being sarcastic or not, but I roll my eyes anyway because he's a prick.

I get back around the counter and ask Carol if she's good. "All good, Boss Lady!" she replies with a wink.

I go about my day, definitely *not* thinking about Ethan. We just kissed. It's fine. I still hate him. He's still ruining my life. He's still going to leave. Plus, I'll meet chaiguy87 soon, and it feels promising. I know we've only messaged, but I have a good feeling about him.

Jess comes down to the café by mid-afternoon, and you'd never know she was sick the night before. She's gorgeous, her hair curled like an old-school movie star. She's wearing one of the two dresses I own, and where it looks like a paper-bag on me, she has added a belt and jacket to make it fit her curves like a glove. The jacket and shoes are from last night, but you can't even tell. She's not even remotely doing a walk of shame.

"Hey, babes!" she says to me and Carol.

Carol smiles widely. "Well hi, Little Boss. Need an iced tea?"

"Nah, I'm good. I stayed with Sarah last night. She brought me a tea earlier." She smiles wide and radiant, white teeth practically glowing.

"Did you use my whitening strips?" I point and yell at her.

"Oops, gotta go! Was just coming to say bye. My ride is here; love you so much! Kisses!" she shouts as she runs out the door.

I look out the front windows and see her climb into Liam's stupid car, and I'm not even remotely surprised. I shake my head and glance at Carol.

"Don't look at me, toots. She ain't my sister!" Carol shakes her head too and walks away laughing.

By the time we close, I'm exhausted. Bone deep tired. I barely slept a wink last night, so I make my way up to my place, shower, and crash.

I wake up around four in the morning with the intention of taking a morning walk before we open, but it's raining *again*. I decide to head downstairs and work on inventory instead. When I get to my office in the café, I realize I haven't checked my messages from chaiguy87. I open it up on my laptop and read his last message.

It's short and to the point. No conversation, just a request to meet sooner. I really can't blame him for wanting to meet sooner . . . In my last message to him, I admitted I had kissed someone else. I know he probably doesn't care. We haven't met. He doesn't even know what I look like. I'm sure he just wants to meet to find out where my head is at and if we *actually* find each other attractive.

I type out a response:

> *Chaiguy87,*
> *Would love to. How's tomorrow at The Poppy Pub in Rose Point at 7 p.m.?*
> *It's near Rose Point Books and near where my sister will be that night, in case you turn out to be a serial killer. <3*
> *XOXO, Coffeegal13*

I press send before I can talk myself out of it. This was always the plan. We were always going to meet, but I'm still nervous. It's the combination of not knowing what he will look like and not knowing if he's been honest through our messages.

What if we can't hold a conversation in person? What if it isn't as easy when we are face-to-face? What if he doesn't make me smile like his messages do?

I try not to think about it too much as I go about my day. Those are tomorrow Sarah's problems.

cHaPTer THirTy-THree

Ethan

SARAH ANSWERED. I WAKE up to a message back asking to meet tomorrow, and I let out a sigh of relief. When I didn't hear from her yesterday, I started to worry.

About what, I'm not quite sure. All I know is I need to explain now, before her feelings for what she thinks are two different men develop into something more. I feel like I'm risking breaking her heart twice right now, because I can't possibly stay in Daisy Ridge, can I?

It's something I've been dwelling on all morning.

Liam can tell I'm distracted as we head out. He snaps his fingers in front of my face. "Earth to Ethan. You okay, bro?"

"Yeah, just thinking. Sorry," I mumble.

"Ha! Thinking is overrated, man. Just *be*," he says tapping his steering wheel to the music.

I will be so grateful when I don't have to work with him anymore. I'll be eternally happy to never be in this car again either.

He pulls up to Daisy Ridge Coffee Co., and my stomach does a somersault. I haven't seen Sarah since the kiss. Since Jess got drunk and stopped me from pushing Sarah too far. I know where that kiss was heading. I could feel how much she wanted more. It was an odd feeling. I've never been able to just tell like that. I was so in tune with her body that night, and I've thought about it over a hundred times in the last twenty-four hours.

We get out of Liam's car and head in. It's fairly busy. Carol and Sarah are working hard. We wait in line a bit longer than usual because it's so packed. When we finally reach the register, Carol takes our orders.

"I'll do an iced Maple Brown Sugar Latte please." I smile at Carol.

She tilts her head at me. "Really? No Dirty Chai?"

"Nah, I'm going to mix it up today." I look over her shoulder at Sarah, who has her back to me. She's making drinks and chatting with the people waiting.

"Eyes on me, sweetheart, I'm the one taking your order." Carol grins and winks at me.

Oh lord. If there is one thing I've learned over the past few weeks in Daisy Ridge, it's that Carol is a loose cannon.

She starts laughing. "You should see your face." She lets out a sigh and then takes Liam's order. He still orders his large iced Sarah's Special.

I pay today. Liam and I have been taking turns. I leave a tip, and Carol winks at me again as we walk away.

"What a hoot that lady is. I like her," Liam says, "I wonder how she'd be in bed . . . "

"Dude, she's like double your age," I tell him.

"Like that's stopped me before," Liam boasts.

I gag, and he laughs.

We wait a few minutes for our drinks, and I admire Sarah the entire time. She creates delicious beverages for everyone while making easy conversation with them. She makes eye contact with everyone and gives each person their own individual moment to start their day. It's amazing to watch.

Her hair is up with her signature claw clip, today's oversized tee sports a kitten with a giant heart, and her leggings are, surprisingly, not black. She has on red leggings that match the giant heart on her shirt perfectly.

Liam is chatting with some girl he met the other day next to me, and he introduced me, but I couldn't tell you her name or what she looks like. My eyes can't leave Sarah. It's mesmerizing to watch her create drinks so flawlessly.

She calls out our names, and it's finally my turn to steal a second of her attention. I walk up, and her eyes find mine as she continues to make the next drink.

"Hey," I say.

"Hi." She smiles. "You off to destroy my life again today?"

"Not any more than you destroy mine," I respond.

She smiles and then laughs. "What a line, Ethan. What. A. Line."

"Oh, if only you realized it's not a line. It's how I feel." I grab Liam's drink too, give her a smile and a nod, and head off.

When I reach Liam, he is still engrossed in some conversation about a movie with this girl. "Hey, you ready? I got your drink," I say, trying to hand it to him.

"Ah yeah, man. Thanks!" He grabs the drink and then kisses this girl on the cheek and says, "See you later, babe."

We head out the door. "How many girls are you going to date in this town?" I say as we walk toward his car.

"As many as I can," he says with a wide smile. "Listen, they know I'm here temporarily. They know I'm a flirt. They know I'm just here for a good time. I'm not playing anyone. They know I won't commit, and they are fine just taking the ride . . . " He winks at me.

I can't help but wonder if he really is just like that or if it is all some kind of front. He doesn't seem capable of having a *real* conversation with anyone, at least not that I've seen.

We head to the site for a long day at work, and when I get back to the bed-and-breakfast that night, absolutely exhausted, I reply to Sarah.

Coffeegal13,
See you tomorrow at 7 p.m.
I can't wait. I'll be the one in black Converse.
XO, Chaiguy87

It's to the point. I don't want to make things even more complicated than they already are.

I spend the entire next day nervous. I'm not stupid enough to think she won't be mad. I can only hope I've shown her enough of both sides that she ends up understanding.

When I'm nervous, I play a game called worst-case scenario in my head. I think of the worst possible outcome. Unfortunately, in this case, it doesn't make me feel better. The worst-case scenario is Sarah hates me, storms off, and never speaks to me again.

At this point, if Sarah never talked to me again, I think I'd be devastated. The messages as coffeegal13, the tension, the jabs—I've grown to enjoy it all. I don't think I could go back to a life without it.

Being in her presence is the most comfortable place I've ever been.

The day drags as I anxiously wait for the time I can leave and meet Sarah in Rose Point. I look up the The Poppy Pub on my phone. It looks like an intimate bar and restaurant. Not too fancy, but not a dive bar by any means.

It has great reviews, and I'm excited to go check it out. I love exploring the new places around here.

We finally wrap up for the day. I rush back to my room at Lavender Dreams to get ready for the big reveal. I dig through the closet, and I decide to just wear what I'm most comfortable in—jeans, my Red Hot Chili Peppers Graphic Tee, and my black Converse. I bring my solid gray zip up hoodie with me, just like I always do, in case Sarah gets cold.

I head out and make the two-hour drive to Rose Point.

CHAPTER THIRTY-FOUR

Sarah

I'm borrowing Dad's car to drive to Rose Point. Sadly, my fun yellow car is still in Carnation Springs. The latest update from the auto shop yesterday was that they are still waiting for a part to come in. Which naturally, since the car is an artifact, was hard to find and get in stock.

Luckily, Dad doesn't drive much anymore, other than for work. Plus, when I told him it was for a date, he all but jumped up and down with delight. He even hugged me and reminded me that Mom would be proud of me putting myself out there.

He yelled, "Good luck!" as I walked out with his keys, and it was almost enough to make me cry.

It feels like there is so much pressure on this date, mostly because Jess is leaving. I know how that sounds, but without Jess, who do I really have? I know it would make it easier for her to leave if I had someone else to talk to. I want it to be easy for her to leave. This is her dream. I want her to be excited. She said the other day she was worried about leaving me, and I know it's because she thinks I'm lonely.

I also feel an immense amount of pressure because, after over three weeks of messaging, I feel like the conversation should be great. What if the conversation doesn't flow, though? What if he doesn't look like I imagined? What if I'm not attracted to him physically?

I think about it a lot on my long drive to Rose Point. Do I have a type? I don't think I do. When I think about what I do find attractive, though, my mind keeps lingering on Ethan, and that annoys me.

I pull up to meet Jess beforehand. She's smiling and waving at me as I park. I'm parking near The Poppy Pub.

I get out, and she hugs me. "Can you believe I'll live here in three months?" She is adorable and giddy with joy.

"No, I really can't." I smile at her, even though, my heart breaks at the thought. "I'm so proud of you." I squeeze her hand. "How is the apartment hunting going? You and Lindsey having any luck?" I ask, because I know she spent today with her realtor friend and Lindsey looking for places in the city.

"It's going . . . " She looks down at her phone. It feels like she wants to say more, but she hesitates. She finally shrugs her shoulders and says, "Are you excited for your hot date?" She wiggles her eyebrows at me.

"I am excited, but what if he isn't hot?" I laugh nervously.

"Oh, he will be! I think he will *blow* your mind." She smiles, and I laugh at her optimism.

We chat for a few more minutes until she has to head off to grab dinner and drinks with Lindsey. She says they need to make a pros and cons list to go over the places they looked at today.

I give her a giant hug and say, "Wish me luck!"

She releases me and gives me a giant smile. "You don't need luck, Sis. Anyone who knows you is *so* lucky to be a part of your life." She rubs my arm. "Please know, I always want what's best for you. I want you to be happy and for someone to treat you like you're the sun, moon, and all the stars." She sighs. "I've made a few questionable choices lately, but I just . . . know something good when I see it. I just wanted to help, and you've done so much for me. You practically raised me after Mom . . . " Her voice breaks, but she holds it together. "I love you so much. I did something bad, but I promise it was for the best reason." She smiles weakly.

I'm confused, but I'd do anything for Jess. "Whatever it is, I'll help you through it. We can do anything together," I remind her, and I give her another big hug. "I love you, Jess. We will figure out whatever is bothering you! But I have to go, or I'll be late! I'll call you after!"

"I'm hoping there isn't an *after*. I'm hoping it goes *all night*." She winks at me.

I laugh. "Probably not. It's only a first date!" I yell at her as I walk away.

"Yeah, about that . . . Remember how much I love you!" she yells back. I'm confused again by her comment, but I don't have time to ask questions now, so I hustle down the sidewalk to The Poppy Pub. I've only been there once, but it was the perfect vibe. It's covered in florals, greenery even hangs from the ceiling. The walls and decor are black and white, with pops of pink, orange, and red flowers. The lighting is intimate, and the last time I was here, it just felt like the perfect place for a first date someday.

My stomach is in knots; my palms are sweaty. I don't get this giddy feeling about dates usually. I'm so excited, it might even be hard for me to eat.

I take a deep breath, open the front door, and walk in. I'm immediately excited by the smell of garlic bread. I look down toward the floor to try and find a man with black Converse shoes . . . I find a pair near the bar and anxiously look up to see the face paired with them.

But . . . it's Ethan.

It's Ethan.

I stand there staring at his face, not sure what to do or what is happening. Is Ethan . . . Chaiguy87? That can't be right. I *like* Chaiguy87, and I hate Ethan.

I think back to the messages—Chaiguy87 hates his job and worked in a coffee shop. Ethan *did* take over making coffee that one day I was sick with extreme ease. I never even questioned the how or why.

Chaiguy87 orders a different drink and mixes it up. Ethan has ordered three different drinks in the time I've known him.

Chaiguy87's go-to is an iced Dirty Chai, and that's the drink Ethan has ordered the most.

My brain still won't process, though, Ethan can't be Chaiguy87. Ethan is a total jerk.

Ethan's eyes finally find mine, and he turns to grab a bouquet off the seat next to him. They look oddly familiar, and as he walks over toward me, all the pieces fall into place.

Jess *just* told me she did something bad for a good reason. When I said it was a first date, she made that weird comment. This is all a setup.

Now I'm pissed. Did this man just lie to me *again*?

Ethan must notice the rage taking over my face, because he slows his steps and looks hesitant to come closer. When he finally gets close enough, he holds the flowers out toward me.

"You look beautiful, Sarah." He smiles nervously.

"Did you know?" I seethe.

"I did. I promise it changes nothing. I'm still chaiguy87," he whispers.

"So you made a fool of me *again*?" I practically spit at him.

"No, oh god. No, Sarah. I've never made a fool of you, and I would never. I think the world of you." He reaches for me, but I turn away and walk out the door.

I get to the sidewalk and frantically look around for a bench or my car . . . Just somewhere to breathe for a second. Ethan walks out and yells, "Sarah, please wait!" as I start running down the sidewalk. I turn a corner and find a bench.

I sit for a second to compose myself. I put my face in my hands and rub at my eyes. The stinging behind them is unnecessary. I'm not going to cry over this man. That's silly. It's not like it's love or anything.

I talked to some stranger on the internet, and I kissed Ethan the other night. We've been on one blind date. This isn't something to cry about. I need to keep it together.

I hear footsteps approaching next to me. I look up to see Ethan's remorseful face.

"Please don't. Don't look at me with that pity," I hiss.

"I don't pity you, Sarah. I admire you. Jess helped me after our fiasco because I *liked* you. I had never felt such a strong connection, such a magnetic pull to a woman before you, and I don't think I ever will again if I'm being perfectly honest." He gives a weak smile.

"I knew you'd be upset when you found out. It's why I wanted to move this up. After we kissed the other night and you confessed you felt guilty, I couldn't keep talking to you as Chaiguy87. I needed you to know. The guy you liked on screen and the guy you hate but kissed any-way—they are the same."

He sets the bouquet down next to me on the bench.

"Jess helped me out and made the same bouquet you had in Daisy Ridge Coffee Co. the day I met you. White lilies. I can't look at white lilies now without thinking about how . . . how I think I knew you were special the moment I saw you. The moment you huffed and puffed, looking for hot coffee sleeves. I just . . . I don't know, Sarah. I knew you'd be upset, but I needed a chance to tell you. I don't *want* to be opening a Starbucks near your beautiful coffee shop. I wish I could stop it. I wish I could help you with your business. I hate my job, and quite honestly, I kind of hate Liam. The past few weeks, though, I haven't minded my job because it keeps me close to you. Close to you is my favorite place to be." He sighs, and takes a step back. "I'm going to head back to our table. It looks like you need a minute, but I hope you come back in and join me for our date. Let me explain more. I'll wait fifteen minutes, but if you're done with this, if you're too upset. I understand." He gives me a small, weak smile and walks away.

I sit there staring after him, wondering what the fuck to do next.

CHAPTER THIRTY-FIVE

Ethan

I GAVE IT MY all.

It's the only thing in my life I've given 100 percent to in a long time. I have no regrets, except for maybe not telling Sarah on that first blind date what I was in town for. Honestly, though, if I had, that story wouldn't seem right for us. I think we were meant to have a different story. This one may be complicated, but it's ours.

At least that's what I tell myself while I wait . . .

I sit and wait fifteen minutes, hoping she will be okay with this. Hoping she will come and give me a chance, but fifteen minutes pass, and I wait another five just in case. At this point, I have to give up the table. I leave some cash on the table and leave.

It's devastating to walk out, to leave the delicious smell of Italian food along with all my hopes and dreams at the table.

I get to my car and text Jess.

> Didn't go well, she didn't come back.
> Thanks again for all your help.

> She will! She will come around! Give
> her some time!!!! <3

I don't think she will. I think this really is the end.

I tried my best, though. It's what my dad would always say: If you tried your best, then you can't do anymore and you'll live with no regrets.

I make the long drive back to Daisy Ridge in silence. I don't even turn the music on. I just keep picturing Sarah singing "Espresso" in the passenger seat or laughing in the rain with the top down.

When I make it back to my room, I head inside. I don't even take off my clothes, just my shoes, and I face plant onto the grandma quilt that adorns my bed and groan into it. It's still dark in my room, but why even bother turning on the lights? I'll probably just lay here questioning my existence for the next few hours until I fall asleep.

It's only been a few weeks, so why do I care? It's the question on repeat in my head right now. I groan again, roll onto my back, and stare at the ceiling and wonder what I'll do now. Sarah has consumed all my thoughts the past few weeks here in Daisy Ridge. I guess now I'll just have to focus on work.

I hate work.

Sarah gave me something to look forward to; she made me smile after almost a whole year of feeling like I may never smile again.

I lay there thinking about leaving this floral bed-and-breakfast and heading home. Except home doesn't feel like a place that even exists anymore.

I'm deep in my thoughts when I'm startled by a loud knock on the door. "UGGGHHHHHHHH!" I shout loudly, loud enough that I hope Liam can hear it from the other side of the door. I truly cannot handle talking to Liam right now. It's the worst possible time. I lift myself off the springy mattress and aggressively swing open the door. I start to say, "Liam, I can't—" But I'm shocked to see Sarah standing on the other side.

"Hi," she whispers.

"Hi," I reply.

She stares at me for a second, opens her mouth, and then closes it.

She sighs. "I'm still pissed."

"I understand," I say with a smile.

"Then why are you smiling?" She glares as she crosses her arms in front of her.

"Because you're here. I told you, for whatever reason, close to you is my favorite place to be." I pause. "Do you want to come in? It's kind of a grandmother-looking room, but if you're cold . . . " My voice trails off.

"I need you to tell me something first," she states.

"Anything," I say as I lean against the door frame.

"Why?" she questions.

"Why what?" I say.

"Why'd you do it? Why'd you ask Jess to set up the emails? Why go to the extreme?" she says quietly.

"I just . . . " I sigh. "It's hard to put into words. I feel this draw toward you. I knew as soon as our first date ended I had completely messed up. I should've told you why I was in town, what my job was. You had *just* started smiling and laughing, though, and I didn't want it to end. Your laugh was the best sound I'd ever heard, and I wanted to hear it more. I was already so pissed about my job. I just . . . I wanted to forget about it for the night and be myself with you. As soon as I dropped you off, I realized I fucked up. I should've told you. So I asked you on the second date, mostly because I really did want to get to know you more. I wanted to hear you laugh and see you smile again, but also because I wanted to tell you why I was in town. I wanted to explain myself."

"I wanted to tell you." He sighs. "I'm almost thirty and don't know what the fuck I'm doing. I hate my job, but it's temporary. I don't know what comes next for me, but I do know the last thing I want to do is fuck up your coffee shop or your life. I think your coffee shop is amazing, Sarah. I think *you're* amazing. Jess could see how much I cared, how much I wanted a chance to explain, but we knew you wouldn't want to hear it. We both knew you wouldn't give me a chance to explain. You're stubborn, and that's a good thing. So Jess and I brainstormed ways I could explain, and when she said one of your favorite movies is *You've Got Mail* . . . And the idea just took hold. Jess wanted to take full responsibility; she wanted to set the whole thing up. She told me to just be myself, write my feelings, and talk with you through email. Her words were literally: Explain your life and hope for the best. So I did."

"I knew you'd be mad when you found out what we did, but I just . . . hoped I'd shared enough that you'd understand where I was coming from. All I could do is hope that you felt this connection too. I don't want to ruin your life, Sarah. I want to be a part of it."

I stare into her eyes, and I can't quite get a read on what she is thinking. Will she walk away again?

She doesn't say anything for what feels like an eternity, and my heart pounds wildly in my chest.

Then she takes a step forward, pushes up on her tiptoes, grabs my shirt in her hands, and kisses me.

CHAPTER THIRTY-SIX

Sarah

I SAT ON A bench for what felt like forever.

I thought of every interaction with Ethan and every message with Chaiguy87. When I realized, I was wrong.

It was hard to admit to myself, but looking back, it was easy to see how I misjudged the situation. I'm still annoyed he didn't tell me on the first date, but I get it. I would have stormed out back then. I can see now how he was probably hoping I would get to know the other parts of him first and talk about the elephant in the room later.

Again, still annoyed, but with everything I know now, how could I not at least just give this a chance? I needed to know why he did it. Why he would go to such an extreme and conspire with my sister?

So I texted Jess and asked which room he was staying in at Lavender Dreams and headed for Daisy Ridge. I threw the very thoughtful bouquet he gave me on the passenger seat and drove as fast as I legally could. I pulled up and stared at the bed-and-breakfast for a long time. I texted Jess again to confirm which room he was in, mostly just to stall some more. I had no idea what I was going to say, but then I finally worked up enough courage to knock—I didn't know what to expect.

Ethan feels that same weird spark I do, that magnetic pull that brings me closer to him. I'm not sure if he gets the pancake flips, butterflies in your stomach feeling, but it doesn't matter.

So I kissed him, and for a split second, I thought maybe it would be terrible and I could forget this whole thing ever happened. I was terribly naïve, though, because I thought the first kiss was the best kiss I'd ever have, and it turns out the second is even better.

He threads his fingers through my hair and kisses me hard. He puts every bit of feeling into it, like if he doesn't, I might float away. He turns me around and shoves me into the wall next to the door, pressing my back there, as the door swings shut. He doesn't take his lips off mine for one single second.

My body is instantly an inferno of need, and while I will recognize it's been a long time for me, it's definitely *more* than I've ever felt with anyone else before.

Every little movement has me aching for more friction. I can't help but squirm against him, trying to press my body as close to his as humanly possible.

He pauses, still holding his hands in my hair, and looks into my eyes. He slides one hand down to my hip and pulls my hair with the other. He kisses along my neck, making his way up before giving my ear lobe a little bite.

I let out a breathy gasp at the unexpected pressure.

"I could literally kiss you forever," he whispers in my ear before kissing the other side of my neck.

"Let's hope you eventually do more than just kiss," I whisper back, and he laughs against my skin. Everything feels so natural with him.

I reach for the bottom of his shirt and pull it up over his head. His chest is gorgeous—all tan and muscular. I run my hands over every single one of the muscles on his chest, and he watches my hands enjoy every inch of him. I look back up at him and smile.

He kisses me again, and I bring my leg up, similar to the last time. This time, though, he reaches down and grabs behind *both* my knees and hurls me up, pressing against me deeper. I can feel him hard against me as I wrap my legs around his hips and twist my ankles together behind him. He groans into my mouth while still feverishly kissing me like his life depends on it.

He holds on to my hips, moving his mouth back down to my neck. I wrap my arms around his neck as he pulls back and looks into my eyes for another second, as if he's scanning my face. He must find whatever he is looking for, because the next thing I know, he's putting his hands under my ass and carrying me over to the bed.

He gently drops me onto the bed while moving on top of me. The springs of the mattress dig into my back, but I don't care. The sensation and pressure of Ethan on top of me is enough to wipe away every thought and feeling within me.

I dig my fingernails into his back as he moves his lips to my collarbone. A moan escapes his lips, gently caressing my skin.

My legs are still wrapped around him as he pushes up on his arms and moves his hand down to the waistband of my pants. He runs one finger along the top of my pants, and I shiver against his touch.

His eyes lock on mine as I lift my ass up, giving him both permission and room to slide my pants down. He practically rips my jeans off in one aggressive movement. My bright red panties greet him, and he runs his finger along the seam of them.

"All this for me?" His eyes practically shimmer in the dark room. I know he can feel how wet I am, how much I *need* this.

I nod.

He licks his lips and then literally rips my red lace panties off and throws them across the room. "You don't need those anymore," he says before he kisses me again. I grab the waist of his pants and pull down hard, taking his boxer briefs with them.

My breath hitches at the sight of his cock. It's . . . huge, and I'm worried I won't be able to handle all of him.

He shimmies out of the rest of his pants and reaches down to the hem of my shirt to pull my top off. He stares at my lace red bra for a long minute. "God, you're perfect," he whispers, kissing me softly before reaching back and removing it in one twist.

He lifts up on his arms to throw my clothes onto the floor, and even though all my clothes are gone, my body is practically on fire.

He presses tender kisses into my skin, starting at my neck and working his way down, exploring every inch of my body.

He presses a kiss to my thigh before grabbing my thighs and lifting up while moving his head down, presses his lips to me and flicking his tongue up along my entrance.

It's been so damn long since someone had their mouth on me like this. I push my arm into my mouth to keep from practically screaming out with pleasure.

He reaches up and grabs my arm to move it down. "Eyes on me, baby," he purrs, and I fucking melt. "I want to hear every sound that comes out of that beautiful fucking mouth." And when he puts his mouth back on me, his tongue quickly finds my clit, and I let out a moan that is practically embarrassing.

He obviously disagrees, though, because I can feel him moan into me. The vibration of him is downright sensational. I feel like a fucking goddess as I grind myself into him more, riding his face like it's my vibrator at home.

My breathing becomes heavy, and my stomach hollows out.

My mind is completely blank as I lay back on the mattress and allow myself to get completely lost in the feeling of his mouth.

I grip the sheets and pull myself up onto my elbows to watch him. He spreads my legs farther, making room for his large body. He lifts his head up, making eye contact for a brief second before spreading me with two fingers and driving his tongue against my clit again in pure ecstasy.

I'm unashamed at this point, because I can feel the pressure building up inside of me, and I'm already ready to release. I'm trying hard not to, but his tongue is magic, putting the perfect amount of pressure and movement against my clit in glorious movements.

He lifts his head up and locks eyes with me. "Let it ride, Sarah. Let me taste your sweet cum, baby. Don't be shy now."

Apparently, that's all my body needed to hear because when his mouth finds me again and he moves back to my clit, all the pressure releases. My toes curl into the sheets, my hands fist the quilt, and I moan Ethan's name like he is everything.

When I come down from my high, Ethan has moved his face up to mine. Eyes on mine, he says, "I could listen to that sound for the rest of my life, and it would never get old. You screamed my name like a fucking prayer." And when he smiles, it's downright incredible.

It could be the world's best orgasm talking, but I think I'm obsessed with this man when he smiles at me like that.

I flip him over onto his back and take him in my mouth. He's too big, though. I use my hand at the base of him and swirl my tongue around the tip. I slowly move up and down his shaft, listening to every breath and moan that comes out of his mouth, finding what brings him the most pleasure. I quicken my pace, move my hands to his muscular thighs, and take him deeper. He groans as he puts his hands in my hair and slowly guides my pace.

Just as I find the perfect rhythm and start to take him even deeper, he moans, and his body twitches. "Dear god, Sarah." He pulls my head up by my hair and meets my eyes. "I'm not ready yet. I need you to get at *least* one more."

I practically burst at just his words alone. I climb up and line up his glorious cock with my entrance. I glance down. I won't lie. I'm slightly intimidated to get all of him inside of me. I look back up, and his eyes are still locked on mine.

"That's it, baby, you've got this. Ride me and take what's yours." He hums.

So I ease down slowly, taking every delicious inch of him, and when I finally get all the way down, I slowly start to move. Grinding into him in slow, concentrated movements.

He looks down at where we meet and moans, "God, look how well you take me." He licks his lips. "Look how fucking sexy you are." His hands find my nipples as he rubs slow circles on them and then gives a small twist. I roll my hips and ride his cock, grinding against him, to find the perfect amount of friction against my clit.

Ethan's hands grip my hips, and his head falls back, eyes closed, as he bites his lip. I roll my hips and repeat that movement over and over, letting the pressure build up deep in my core once again. I moan, "Ethan, fuck you feel so good."

That one statement seems to light a fire within Ethan. He groans and reaches up with one hand and gives my neck a brief squeeze.

"Fuck yes, Sarah," Ethan moans, just as I find my release.

"Ethan, I'm going to . . . " The waves of pleasure wash over me just as he finds his release, too. His body begins spasming, and his cock starts pulsing inside me.

"You're fucking everything," he whispers against my hair, as I collapse onto him. He rubs slow circles against my back.

Chapter Thirty-Seven

Ethan

I FEEL LIKE RON Burgundy in the movie *Anchorman* when he yells, "Veronica and I had sex, and now we are in love!"

Sarah fell asleep quickly after what was possibly the best sex of my life earlier. I haven't gone to sleep yet, though; I'm too nervous this is all a dream. I'm nervous that if I sleep, she will bail.

When she starts to toss and turn, so I rub her back. Her eyes flutter open and meet mine, and she quickly jolts up. "What time is it?" she sleepily gasps.

"It's only one a.m. I was going to wake you up for work. Don't worry!" I say as I keep drawing circles on her back.

"Oh, okay." She sighs as she settles back onto the pillow, her eyes still locked on mine. "Should we . . . talk about this?" she whispers, gesturing between us with her hands.

"Up to you. I know how I feel, and I'm pretty sure you know how I feel. I'm ready to talk whenever you want." I smile at her. I don't want her to feel pressure either way. It's clear to me now where this is going. I just need her to catch up.

Her face pinches with confusion. "Uh, okay," she says quietly. We sit in silence for a while, and I secretly love it.

She's the first person I've ever felt comfortable with in complete silence. I don't feel like I need to fill it with conversation or say something to impress her.

It's part of the reason I loved having sex with her. I'm always overthinking when I am with women, but when I'm with her, everything comes naturally. I say whatever is on my mind.

She smiles at me, and I smile back. "Do you need to shower? Need me to drive you back? Or you can sleep here, and I'll set an alarm?" I whisper, terrified I might scare her off.

She thinks for a second and then smiles. "Want to shower with me?" She scoots off the bed and walks toward the bathroom, damn near taking my entire heart with her.

Her naked body moving in the small amount of moonlight coming through the crappy thin curtains, silhouetting her body in the dark, will be burned into my memories forever.

The shower is intimate. We lather each other with soap, laugh, and make out.

Eventually, I take my fingers and use them to let Sarah find one more release and then wash her off again.

Afterward, Sarah goes home. She says she wants to get a couple hours of sleep in her own bed before work tomorrow.

I can't blame her. This floral bedroom is very overdone, with an absolutely horrendous bed. If I had the choice, I'd move back to my own bed too, especially if it looked as cozy as Sarah's.

I also don't want to seem clingy, so I don't object or try to stop her from leaving. I walk her to the car and kiss her senseless on the hood before watching her drive away.

Hours later now, I haven't slept a single second more, but I feel energized waiting for Liam. I'm secretly hoping he will want to stop at Sarah's along the way to the work site.

Liam walks out of his room with a girl I don't recognize just as a taxi pulls up. He smacks the girl on the butt, she giggles, and then he spins her around and kisses her against the cab. I immediately feel bad for the taxi driver, or do I feel bad for the girl? Maybe both. She giggles again as she climbs in, and he waves after the taxi and finally walks over to me.

Liam stops abruptly at the sight of me. "Dude. You're . . . smiling? I thought you came home alone last night? Did you get some?"

I laugh. "Sometimes it isn't about 'getting some,' Liam . . . "

"Yeah, okay, and coffee isn't about caffeine . . . " He huffs. "You totally got some!" he says as he points at me.

I'm no longer smiling. He's already ruined my perfectly good mood. "Let's go," I say, gesturing to the car.

"Dude, what's the point of being bros if you won't tell me?" he whines.

I roll my eyes at him. When we get in the car, he glances my way. "Sarah's for coffee?" he mutters.

"Sure," I say, trying to play it cool. The last thing I need is him guessing that she is the reason I'm in a good mood this morning.

We make the drive to Sarah's and head inside to find it busy, like usual. As soon as we walk in, though, Sarah's eyes find mine. Almost like she knew I was coming. She gives me a small smile and then continues to make conversation with the current customer.

Liam and I wait in line. When we reach the counter, we are met with a smiling Carol. Today, she is decked out in a lime green fuzzy sweater with coffee mug earrings, and her hair up in a chaotic, curly mess of a bun.

"Well how are my two favorite young men today?" She smirks at us playfully. You really can't help but love Carol.

"We're doing great Carol, thanks," I reply, smiling back at her.

"What's got him so happy today?!" she says to Liam while nodding her head toward me.

"I think maybe he got laid last night," Liam whispers to her, leaning over the counter.

She laughs and playfully swats at Liam. "Well that would likely do it. He was wound up real tight before, wasn't he? You aren't, though," she winks at him. "You get an awful lot of practice, don't you?" She smirks.

"Guys, I'm right here!" I say disgusted.

They both laugh.

"Well, last night must've been a real lucky night, because Sarah was looking well 'taken care of' this morning too!" She grins at us.

Dear lord, no.

Why did she say that?

"OH! YOU DON'T SAY!" Liam practically shouts, glancing my way.

Carol giggles, and I place my order, a honey latte today, and get away from them as fast as I can.

Liam pays faster than ever before, rushing over to come wait with me. A couple of girls try to grab his attention, but he ignores them. Which is a concerning action.

I grab a copy of the Daisy Ridge Gazette off a nearby stand and flip the pages. Avoiding eye contact with Liam at all costs.

"Earth to Ethan," he says as he waves his hand in front of the paper. I glare up at him over the paper. "Are you going to tell me what happened last night? Or should I go ask Sarah?" he whisper-yells at me.

"Dude, I don't know what to say yet. I'm not sure what we are," I whisper-yell back at him. "Just drop it for now, okay? Let her and I figure things out first."

He laughs. "Man, you've got it bad. I'm here for fun. I'm here for all the girls; you . . . you went off and fell in love. Are you going to move to this shithole now?"

"I don't know. It's not love . . . yet," I whisper, more to myself than to Liam.

He laughs as Sarah calls our names out.

We make our way to the counter, and Sarah greets both of us, then continues with, "Have another beautiful day ruining my life." Then she tosses me a wink. She turns and continues to make drinks.

There is a lump lodged in my throat. I was hoping for more from her, not the same usual conversation. I want to say something more, but I don't know what. Sarah's back is toward us, so I accept defeat, grab my drink, and move to leave.

When I glance down, I notice a little note on my cup lid. It reads:

Meet me here at 7—XO coffeegal13

CHAPTER THIRTY-EIGHT

Sarah

SHOULD I HAVE INVITED Ethan here tonight? Probably not, but when I saw him in the café this morning, all I could think about was his tongue and the orgasms, so I wrote a little note on his cup. Now there is no turning back. I'm practically ruined. I'm now addicted to oral sex, and it's all Ethan's fault.

At 6:58, I see Ethan's Jeep pull up. My stomach does actual somersaults. I'm so excited and slightly nervous to see him again, but I'm taking Carol's advice—whether it's a forever love or just a fun fling, I'm going to enjoy this while it lasts.

Carol heads out at seven, and I turn everything off and flip the sign to 'closed.' I walk out and lock the door behind me as Ethan strides up to me. He grabs my face with both hands and kisses me tenderly before whispering, "Hey, you."

I smile up at him. "Hey," I whisper back.

I grab his hand and lead him around back and up the stairs. When we get inside, we are greeted by Trixie, who sidesteps me and heads straight for Ethan. I'm slightly insulted, but I don't let it show.

"Do you like Chinese takeout?" I ask Ethan when we get settled.

"Depends. Is there somewhere in Daisy Ridge that actually has edible food?" he says with a laugh.

I burst into laughter, remembering his gray-ish burger at Delano's. "Yeah, when you live here, you know where the good spots are." I smirk at him while I pull out a menu for our local Chinese takeout restaurant from my junk drawer and hand it to Ethan.

"Will you call so I can rinse off real quick? You can order whatever you want and tell them it's for Sarah's place. They will know. I'll be quick." I smile at him and start walking away. "Oh! And pick a movie, pleaaaseeee!"

"You got it, Boss Lady!" He does a mock salute, and I laugh.

"Oh noooo. That nickname is only for Carol, because she's an *employee*," I point out.

"Well maybe I will be an employee too someday. I think I did a pretty great job filling in while you were sick," he says with a wink.

I don't answer but laugh the whole way to the shower.

I don't bother putting makeup on after I rinse off. Ethan will either like me how I am, or he won't. I don't play the game of trying to impress people.

When I come out in my pajamas, which are basically just a giant graphic tee and plaid pajama pants, Ethan is on the couch scrolling movie options. He does a little double-take when he sees me. "Wow, you clean up nice," he says with a wink. I giggle at the comment.

I waltz over and plop down next to him. I glance at the screen and see *You've Got Mail* ready to play. "Did you want to see if you did it right or something?" I nervously laugh.

He laughs too. "I've actually never seen it," he admits, "but I know the premise. Figured I should give it a watch."

"Seems a little late." I laugh.

"Or is it right on time because I get to watch it with you?" He smiles at me while pressing play.

We watch the first bit of *You've Got Mail* in comfortable silence. One of my favorite things about Ethan is how comfortable I feel around him. There is a knock at the door, and I go grab the Chinese food. The delivery driver hands a gigantic bag over to me as Ethan walks up behind me. He pulls out his wallet and hands the delivery driver cash.

I say, "Thanks so much, Craig. See you next week!" and everyone laughs.

"Weekly occurrence?" Ethan asks.

"Maybe." I smile. "You said yourself there are very few quality food options around here when I don't want to cook!" I defend. "Also you didn't need to pay. I invited you over. I'll get some cash for you."

Ethan grabs my wrist as I start to turn. "No, don't! It's my treat. Plus I think I ordered enough for the US Army. I didn't know what you liked, and I wanted to make sure you had your favorite. Craig was very helpful on the phone. He seems to know your order pretty darn well," he says with a laugh.

We stand there, eyes locked on each other for a minute, when he releases my wrist. I take the bag of food to the couch and set it on the coffee table. I start opening it up and unpacking all the takeout containers.

"Shit, you did order a lot of food." I laugh at Ethan.

"I told you it was a lot!" he grumbles.

"Good thing I'm starving!" I giggle.

We chow down on an enormous amount of Chinese food while watching the movie. It's fun and peaceful. It's probably the most fun I've had with someone besides Trixie in a long time, and we aren't even talking really.

I break open my fortune cookie when Ethan asks, "What does it say?"

I read aloud, "From small beginnings come great things," and laugh. "What does yours say?" I nod my head toward the cookie he just broke open.

He reads, "Wherever you go, go with all your heart." He smiles.

We continue watching the movie. When it ends, I start cleaning up the food, and Ethan helps. "Thanks for inviting me over tonight," he says as we finish cleaning everything up.

"What did you think of the movie? Was it everything you hoped it would be?" I playfully ask him.

"It was even better because I enjoyed it with you," he says, kissing the side of my head and wrapping me in a hug.

For some reason, a hug feels more intimate to me than sex. When he pulls back, I look up at him and kiss him. After a minute, we pull apart.

"Next time, though, we watch *The Fall Guy*. You really sold me on it when we were at Delano's, and I still haven't watched it," I suggest playfully.

He laughs. "Deal. I think you'll love it."

I smile up at him, and a yawn sneaks out.

"Don't be mad, but I got you something," Ethan says.

My stomach drops. "Uhm, we aren't quite there yet, are we?"

He laughs. "It's nothing like that." He pulls his phone out of his pocket and turns the screen to face me.

It's an email. I read it once and then read it again. "Did you get a travel blogger to come to my café? In just a few days?!"

I look up at him in absolute awe.

"I did. I just . . . wanted to help however I could. I told you, Sarah, I want your place to succeed. The last thing I want to do is ruin it, but for now, I'm stuck, and this was something I could do to help." He nervously smiles at me. I take his phone from him and toss it on the couch.

I grab both his hands in mine, press up onto my tip toes, and kiss him.

When we pull apart, I grab his hand and lead him to my room. I push him down onto the bed, place my hands on his knees, and lower myself in between his legs on the floor. I run my hands up his massive thighs and reach for the waistband of his pants. He tilts his hips up, and I yank them down to his knees in one motion, and his cock springs free.

"Sarah, you . . ."

But I take him in my mouth before he can say another word. Ethan's hips move with the surprise, and he lets out a guttural groan followed by an "Oh fuck, Sarah . . . "

I gag a little bit and then spit on him and hit my groove, taking him all the way down my throat.

"Jesus, Sarah," he moans while threading his fingers into my hair.

I slow down and take my time with him, slowly moving up and down his shaft, letting the drool fall freely over it. I twirl my tongue around the tip before reaching a hand down and stroking his balls. He moans, and it fuels me to move faster, taking him as deep as I can.

I bring my hand down to cup his balls gently and continue to palm them while my tongue runs up and down his length. I smile up at him before running my tongue along the underside of his cock.

"Fuck, Sarah," he groans, his legs falling open more. His head falls back, and it makes me eager for more. Knowing I'm making him feel this way is downright powerful.

I swirl around the tip again before taking him deep. I move up and down his shaft slowly.

After a few minutes, he pulls me up by my hair and lifts me from him.

I suck in a sharp breath as he slides his hands down along my body, landing on my waist and gripping the waistband of my pajamas there. Then he slides them down to my ankles and slaps my ass, and I gasp at the shock.

I step out of my pants and get up onto the bed, placing both knees on either side of his waist straddling him.

"Oh fuck no, not yet," Ethan says. "Give me that fucking pussy," he demands, eyes locked on mine.

He grabs my thighs and lifts me to straddle his face. He kisses the inside of both my thighs before running his tongue up me in one long sweep. The initial shock of his mouth on me sends waves of pleasure over my body, goosebumps pebbling across my skin. He moves his tongue inside me, finding that perfect pace before sucking on my clit.

He moans into me, and I feel like my body might combust.

I need more, so I push myself off his mouth and flip around to take him back into my mouth. He grabs my ass and brings me back down to straddle his mouth again. I swirl my tongue around the tip of him before going all the way down as he moans into me while driving his tongue against my clit. With each expert stroke of his tongue, I feel the pressure continue to build in my core.

He moves back to kiss my thigh again. "Who do you think will come first? My bet is on you."

A shiver runs up my spine before I mumble an "Oh fuck!" around his cock and grip his thighs tight. I love a good competition, but I'm definitely fucking losing this one. I roll into him more and ride his face as my body begins to shake. I close my eyes and try to put all of my focus on him. I lick up his shaft and around the tip before taking him deep into the back of my throat again. It's no use, though. Ethan just knows my body. He's completely in tune with what I want. He greedily grabs my ass with both hands, forcing me into him even more, before sucking my clit in between his teeth.

I tremble against him, the pressure building, rocking against his face. I circle my tongue around his head while gripping his shaft in my hand. I spin my tongue in circles around the tip of him and slowly move my hand up and down.

"Fuck, Sarah, yes," Ethan moans into me. As I moan around his tip. Ethan's hips start to move like he may need more. I take him deep to the back of my throat again. For a second I gag on him, and he mumbles, "I love it when you gag on me."

I use my saliva to fuck him with my hand, and Ethan grips my ass again tight with both hands.

He puts more pressure against my clit, and my legs violently shake around him.

I bite my lip as I moan, having a full-blown out-of-body experience as I climax. Ethan moans something into me as waves of pleasure roll through me. I dig my nails into his thighs so hard, I'm afraid I'm breaking skin.

When I come down from the high I'm riding, Ethan lifts me up off his face and slides me down him, lining me up with his cock from behind. "I knew you would come first." I can hear the cockiness in his voice. "You ready for another one, baby? Ride me."

I line him up at my entrance and slowly move down one inch, teasing him slightly.

He smirks at me and hums, "Good god, Sarah. Just take it, baby."

I move down, taking inch by inch of him into me, stretching and letting him fill me slowly. When I get all the way down, I take a deep breath and begin to slowly ride him. Ethan thrusts, and I moan while rolling my hips and moving in slow, concentrated movements.

He groans, "Oh fuck, Sarah. Oh god, not yet. I need more of you." He pulls me off him, sits up, and spins me around, pinning me onto the bed, taking a moment to kiss down my neck. He grabs both my hands in his, moving them up above my head and pinning them there. Ethan moves back into me and continues with a slow yet exhilarating pace, building pressure within me again.

I shout with pleasure, "Fuck, Ethan! Damn it, you feel so good."

He moves into me and continues with repetitive satisfying movements over and over. The fullness and the way we fit together so perfectly and the perfect angle of my clit moving against him, creates a perfect storm. I start rocking my hips as my climax begins to build once again.

He lets go of my hands and moves them down the length of my body. My head falls back, and I reach up and wrap my arms around his neck.

My eyes start to close when Ethan snaps, "I said, eyes on me. I want to see every expression on that gorgeous face."

He reaches down and grips my ass in his hands, lifting me up slightly, and drives into me at the perfect angle. I combust again. The second orgasm nearly takes me all the way out. Ethan continues to thrust into me, finding his release too, and we ride out the spasms and shockwaves of our orgasms together.

When we come down, he whispers against my neck in a mess of heated breath, "You have no idea what you fucking do to me."

CHAPTER THIRTY-NINE

Ethan

I THINK I'VE DIED and gone to heaven.

That's my first thought when I look over at Sarah and see her smiling, satisfied face next to me on her bed.

"I think I'm in love with your tongue," she says to me while laughing. She looks happy and content, and my heart flutters slightly at the view.

"I *know* I'm in love with your mouth." I laugh and sit up. Laying down next to her is the happiest I've been in forever. She glances over at me. I rub my thumb over her bottom lip, and I roll onto my side to kiss her gently.

"What about when my mouth is snarky and puts you in your place?" she questions.

"Especially when it's snarky and puts me in my place," I whisper, and she smiles even wider.

"You up for another shower?" she says, reaching for my hand and pulling me up. We rip off the clothes that still remain and climb into the shower. I wash her, and she washes me, and if I'm being honest . . . I never liked sharing a shower before. It felt cramped and cold, but with Sarah . . . well, we just work.

I kiss her into the shower wall after we are all cleaned off and eventually place one finger inside her. She gasps at the shock. Then I turn her around and take her from behind while the hot water glides across our skin, and we end up having to wash all over again.

I stayed at Sarah's all night, and very little sleep happened. After another steamy shower session, we went to sleep, only for me to wake up at three a.m. to Sarah stroking me.

By 4:30, she had made me coffee in the café, and I headed back to my room at Lavender Dreams to get ready. I already miss Sarah and her warmth, which is absolutely ridiculous since it's only been a few hours.

I'm drinking the delicious drink she made me, some kind of raspberry mocha or something. Honestly, I'm not usually a fan of fruit flavors in my coffee, but of course Sarah made it work.

I forwarded her the email with the information on the travel blogger coming in just a couple days. I'm waiting for Liam out in front of our bed-and-breakfast, and I can't believe we only have another eight days here in Daisy Ridge. The crew will take over after that, and construction should be completed in about five weeks. When it's complete, Liam and I will have to come back to do walk-throughs and such, but for five weeks, we have to move on to our next project.

I'm a mess just thinking about it. Things *finally* took off with Sarah, and honestly, she feels like the one. That probably sounds dumb, but when you know, you know, right? At least, that's what people always say . . .

Liam strolls out, unusually late today, he takes one look at me and starts laughing.

"What time did you get back?" he asks.

"I have no idea what you're talking about," I say, holding my chin high.

"Dude, you're literally holding a cup of coffee from Sarah's," he says gesturing to the cup in my hand.

"Shit," I say looking down.

He laughs. "Dude, it's fine. I'm happy for ya. Is this like it for you now, though? You moving here?"

"I don't know, man. She's different. She's special. I'm comfortable and happy with her . . . I just . . . all I know is, my cheeks hurt after I spend time with her from smiling so much, and I've never felt like that before," I mumble. "I don't know. I gotta get through this job until Eric can take it, though."

Liam nods. "I can't say I understand, because I'd keep this job. It's good money; it's easy . . . and Daisy Ridge is meh, but like, if you're happy, you just gotta do what's best for you, or whatever."

It's the first intelligent thing Liam has ever said to me. I'm shocked to say the least. I feel like he can tell things are different for me. Which gives me this odd feeling of hope. Maybe I'm not crazy, and maybe everything will work out.

Liam nods to the car. "Can we still go to Sarah's, though? I need coffee stat, bro." And just like that, he's back to being a douche.

"Yeah, man, let's go. I'll drive today." We climb in my Jeep and head off for the only person I want to see.

It's another busy morning for Sarah when Liam and I get there. Honestly, it makes me hopeful that Starbucks won't ruin her business too much. I think there is enough room for both in this town. I'm also hoping the travel blogger will provide the little boost Sarah might need to get through the opening six weeks from now.

On the bulletin board in the corner, I notice a sign that wasn't there yesterday. It reads: *Help Wanted, inquire with Sarah.* On the bottom, it has her phone number listed.

The older gentleman who resembles jolly old Saint Nick is ordering at the register with Carol. They keep talking forever, and Carol is rubbing his arm and winking at him.

Sarah turns while making drinks and yells "Smithy! Move it or lose it! I love you, but you're holding up the line!"

She makes eye contact with me, and my heart skips a beat when she winks at me. Smithy moves over, yelling back, "Sorry, Sarah dear. Miss Carol is just too darn pretty these days." Carol giggles as we move up to the register.

"Aw, now, Carol, I thought I was your favorite boy . . . " Liam teases.

"Now, now. I said the other day, you're my favorite *young* boy. That man over there is my favorite *old* boy." She looks over to Smithy and winks. The redness on his neck creeps all the way up to his cheeks, and I still can't help thinking he looks a bit like Santa Claus.

I glance back over at Sarah who is expertly making drinks and schmoozing her customers. I tell Carol to write 'Sarah surprise' on the cup—I want her to make whatever she wants for me today. Those drinks have been my new favorite.

When my order is ready, I walk up and brush hands with Sarah as she hands me the cup. She smiles. "It's a gingerbread latte. Enjoy," she says with a smirk. "Have another wonderful day ruining my life boys!" she yells out to Liam and I as we walk out the door.

The next two days pass in a blur. I'm running on little to no sleep, but I don't mind at all. I work all day, stay up late watching movies with Sarah, usually doze off, and then wake up with Sarah at around 3:00. Turns out she's a morning sex kinda gal, and I don't hate it. There is something about the early morning haze with Sarah that is pure fucking magic.

I hate to use the word love, but it kinda feels like I might be falling in love with her. Being with her is like that first sip of a delicious coffee in the morning. My cheeks still hurt from smiling so much when I'm around her.

When it's finally the day of the travel blogger's visit, Sarah and I are up extra early. I offered to help her clean and prep so we can make sure her café is the best it's ever looked. Jess comes in early to refresh the centerpieces and creates beautiful floral arrangements. Carol arrives just before opening, wearing her pink cheetah print with her hair curled so much it almost looks like an afro.

I text Liam and tell him I'll meet him at the job site after I wrap up here, and he sends a single thumbs-up emoji in return.

Around 9:00 a.m., @southwesttraveler walks in. I actually don't know her real name, but she looks exactly like I expected. Her hair and makeup are done to perfection. She's wearing a pink athletic wear set, like she's going to go work out after this, but based on her hair and makeup, it's highly unlikely. She carries a tripod along with a camera bag and smiles broadly as she walks in! "Well hellooooooooo, handsome! You must be Chaiguy87?" She gestures to me with her free hand.

"Hi, yes! My name is Ethan. This is Sarah, the owner of Daisy Ridge Coffee Co." I motion toward where Sarah stands next to me. She looks nervous, but she is smiling. She did her hair and makeup today, so she looks different from the Sarah I know and love, but she's still wearing her usual oversized tee and leggings. Today's T-shirt is plain, though, solid black with a gray long sleeve underneath. Her well-loved high-top black Converse are proudly on display, though, as she shakes the hand of the travel blogger.

"Hi! I'm Tracee," she finally says, "Nice to meet you! I'm so excited to be here! I had no idea you were out this way, but my fans are going to love somewhere cute to stop on their way to Carnation Springs and Rose Point! EEK! I'm already so stoked to share!" She literally jumps up and down clapping her hands together before pausing and putting her things down. "Okay, so I'm totally going to add you to the girl's trip itinerary on my website! It's a huge hit and gets thousands of clicks per week. Lots of girlies are planning getaways to Carnation and Rose these days!"

She starts aggressively setting up multiple cameras.

"Just go about your normal day. I'm going to get some footage of your everyday routine, and then I'll interview each of you in a bit!" She smiles, turns to me, and winks. "You wanna go first, handsome?"

"Oh, I actually don't work here. I was just setting this whole thing up for my . . . Sarah . . . " I stumble over my words, wanting to call her my girlfriend but remembering we haven't talked about anything. I also feel like 'girlfriend' is too low-key for how I feel about her at this point.

"Oh! That's so stinking sweeeeeet!" she screeches. "I still totally want to interview you if that's ok?! Like as a customer?!" she asks.

"I guess, if it's fine with Sarah?" I look Sarah's way, and she looks overwhelmed and confused.

She mumbles, "Yeah, that's good . . . fine."

"YAY! OKAY!" Tracee yells as she begins filming. Sarah moves behind the counter and starts making drinks flawlessly while Tracee films it.

It's fun to watch. I stay for two hours while Tracee gets everything she needs. She interviews Carol for far longer than Sarah is comfortable with. I can tell because she is picking at her nails aggressively. Her telltale sign that she's nervous. Eventually, she interviews Sarah. Everything seems to go super smoothly. The customers coming in are excited by the camera presence. Tracee picks a couple of random locals to say a few words about Daisy Ridge Coffee Co.

When Tracee is ready to interview me, she takes me outside to film in front of the store. She asks a few questions about the coffee and which drinks I enjoy. I tell her my favorites and then share that my new favorite is whatever Sarah wants to make me.

"Just one more question, handsome. What do you love most about Daisy Ridge Coffee Co.?" she smiles at me and moves her tiny mic toward me.

That's an easy one. "Everything. Literally everything. Daisy Ridge Coffee Co. makes you feel instantly comfortable. The owner, Sarah, has put her life and soul into this coffee shop, and it shows as soon as you walk in the door. I love the atmosphere, drinks, and people who work here." I smile at her.

"That was perfect! Thank you!" Tracee smiles at me and directs me back inside.

Sarah still looks nervous.

Tracee comes over to let us know she has finished up filming all her content. When she comes over to me, she says, "Thank you *so* much for sending me the info about this place! It's the absolute cutest, and I think it's definitely going to be a big hit on my website!"

"Thank *you*! We really appreciate you getting the word out." I smile and reach my hand out to shake hers.

Tracee heads out to leave, and Sarah comes around from behind the counter. "How do you think it went? Seemed good right?" she asks me nervously.

I reach down and take her hand in mine. "I think it went really well, sweetheart." I press a kiss to her knuckles.

CHAPTER FORTY

Sarah

I ALWAYS KNEW THIS was going to be temporary. I told myself when I got involved that it was just a fun time, not a forever love.

For some reason, though, my heart can't seem to catch up with my head. He's leaving today for his next job. He'll be back in five weeks to do a final walk-through on the construction site. So the good news is this isn't a final goodbye; it's an 'I'll see you in five weeks.'

That's a bit easier to handle at the moment, but I'm definitely worried for my heart five weeks from now.

For the past week, I've spent every free minute I've had with Ethan. Watching movies, playing card games, cooking, eating, baking, going for walks, and even talking about books. He read *Heir of Sun and Moon* by Jenessa Ren since I told him I loved it. We had the most fun discussion about it and even made a plan on discussing book two when he comes back to town. It's giving me something to look forward to because I can't wait to hear what he thinks about the next cliffhanger.

I'm finishing up my closing tasks but taking my sweet time because I'm slightly dreading what comes next . . . Every task brings me closer to having to say goodbye to Ethan as he heads off for his next project. Honestly, he should've headed out earlier today, and I know the only reason he is making the long, late night drive is for me.

I walk around and make sure everything is prepped and ready for tomorrow. I want the café to be perfect because I have interviews for a new employee. I prep everything I can so Carol and I don't fall behind during my interviews. I only have a couple of months until Jess leaves, and I need to make sure I have a new employee trained well before then.

I turn off the lights and head out front to lock up. Ethan's Jeep is sitting out front, and my stomach plummets. I run across the parking lot to Ethan and leap into a big hug. I squeeze him tight in my arms. "Are you sure you have to go?" I whisper.

"Yeah, sweetheart, but it's only for five weeks." He kisses the top of my head gently while rubbing circles on my back.

I feel a stinging behind my eyes but blink and fight them off. He's just a guy, and this was just a fun fling. It was short; there is no reason to cry. I swallow the huge lump in my throat to keep the tears at bay.

"It's only five weeks," he whispers, and the repetition feels like it is more for him than me.

"I've had the best time with you." I smile up at him, resting my chin on his chest.

"You are my happy," he whispers, and then he lazily kisses me. It's slow and full of meaning. It's a promise and a goodbye.

I pull him tighter against me as we kiss.

I release him and take a step back, looking up at him. "I wish you were coming up for dinner."

"Me too." He smiles. "I'll message you when I get to my new hotel; here's hoping it's a little less 'old lady-ish' than the one I had here."

I laugh. I'll secretly miss that crazy teapot of a room. "See you soon," I whisper, giving his hand a squeeze.

"See you soon." He presses a kiss to the top of my head, walks over to his car, and drives away.

I watch his red Jeep drive off, and my heart cracks slightly just as I finally let a tear fall.

I stand there for a full minute after he's gone, staring at the road he drove down, which is now empty. I sigh and finally head up to my apartment. There is a bouquet of white lilies by the door.

Attached is a note. "See you on the screen, Coffeegal13" with a little hand drawn heart and the letter *E*.

My stomach has butterflies as I rush inside and bust open my laptop. I log in to the email Coffeegal13, which I haven't logged into since the day I met Ethan in Rose Point as Chaiguy87.

There are fifteen unread emails.

The first one is from the morning after we first had sex, it reads:

> *You are pure happiness.*
>
> *The comfort and joy I feel when I'm with you is in-describable.*
>
> *Thanks for giving me a second (or is it a third?) chance.*
>
> *XO, Chaiguy87*

There are a dozen more throughout our time together, ranging from how beautiful I look to describing how he feels after our dates, and there is even one about the night we ate Chinese and how it was the happiest night he has had in a decade.

My heart cracks a little more with each email I read.

When I get to the most recent email, it's dated one hour ago. It reads:

> *Coffeegal13,*
>
> *I'll never be able to put into words how much the last few weeks have meant to me or how much Daisy Ridge has changed my life. How much you have changed my life.*
>
> *I know the next five weeks will be hard for us, but I promise I will make it easier by writing to you every day. I'm going back to our roots and letting you ask all the questions you want. <3*
>
> *Please know that over the next five weeks, I'll be consumed with thoughts of you and your mouth. (The*

conversation, snarky remarks, and *its talented blowjob abilities) ;)*
   Forever yours, Chaiguy87

I sit and smile at the screen for a long time. Five weeks is nothing in the grand scheme of life. I can make it five weeks, and maybe if we are chatting along the way, we can figure something out. Maybe we can be long distance in the end? Or maybe, I don't know. All I know is, I'm not ready to let this thing with him go quite yet. So for the next five weeks, I'm going to chat with him and focus on my business. I'm going to make Daisy Ridge Coffee Co. *the* place to be.

Tracee should be sharing her blog post featuring Daisy Ridge Coffee Co. soon along with all the content she shot during her visit. I want to be ready with a new employee before then.

I'm going to hire someone and get my butt in gear. I think if I focus hard enough on my job and making sure Daisy Ridge Coffee Co. is the best it can be, time might just pass pretty quickly.

There is a knock on my door, and for a minute, my heart leaps, because I briefly think it might be Ethan. My head catches up, though, and logically, I know it isn't.

I get up and run over to the door, and when I fling it open, Jess is standing there with my favorite bottle of chardonnay smiling.

"Thought you may need some company tonight!" she says.

"From you? Of course! We only have a couple months left of this . . ." I smile weakly at her.

I move over so she can come inside.

"We can still do this after I move; just not as spur of the moment . . . " She sighs. "I know it won't be the same, though."

"Hey!" I grab her hand in mine. "It'll be the same in every way that matters, you can't get rid of me." I smile at her. "Let's watch a movie—you need to see *The Fall Guy*!" I pull her over to my couch and push her down. "I'll grab glasses and a bottle opener."

I grab the supplies and a ton of snacks and make my way over to the couch.

We snack, laugh, drink the whole bottle of wine, and cuddle.

It's perfect. This is what I've been missing with Jess. We've both been so busy lately; we haven't made time for this.

The movie ends, and Jess has her head on my shoulder. She whispers "You were right; it was a good movie."

I laugh. "I can't take credit. Ethan told me to watch it, and I didn't. Not until we watched it together." I smile weakly at the memory.

Jess sits up and looks over at me. "What's going on with you two? Are you . . . doing long distance? Was this whole thing just a fling?"

"I don't know. I told myself it was temporary and just for fun . . . but . . . my heart hasn't got the memo I guess. I already miss him, which probably sounds weird and pathetic . . . " I groan. I flop my hand across my face to hide my embarrassment from Jess.

She grabs my hand. "It's not weird or pathetic, Sarah, I helped him for a reason. I saw something special there. I saw it on the first blind date, even when you didn't. You guys fit; you work. I think you should work for it or fight for it. Don't give up yet if you aren't ready."

I smile at her. "It's not entirely up to me, but I'm not deciding anything until I see him again in five weeks. In the meantime, I'm focusing on the business. I need to kick it into high gear before the Starbucks opens, and I need to hire someone new before my baby sis leaves me to go follow her dreams." My eyes get glossy looking at her.

"I may be leaving, but I'll always be just a phone call away, and I'll always be your friend too. Sisters or not, you're also my best friend. Well, you and Lindsey . . . " She laughs.

"Yeah, well hate to break it to you, but it turns out Carol is actually my bestie for the restie." We both burst out laughing.

"Let's go to bed!" I smile at Jess. "I've got to be up early."

CHAPTER FORTY-ONE

Ethan

I DRIVE AWAY FROM Sarah's, and I'm immediately upset.

It's silly. We really haven't known each other long enough for me to feel like my heart is cracking open with every mile I drive away from Daisy Ridge.

I'm just upset that I got thrown into this job, and I haven't worked through or processed *why* I got thrown into this job. I've put my head down and tried my best for my family, because they need me to do this.

With Sarah, I felt like myself for the first time since my dad passed. If I'm being honest . . . I actually felt like myself for the first time . . . ever.

I call Liam on speaker phone in the car.

"Hey, man!" he answers.

"Hey, just wanted to let you know that I'm just now leaving!" I say.

He laughs. "Took you long enough. What did you need a quickie for the road or something like that?"

"Nah, I just needed to say goodbye alone . . . " My voice trails off.

"Whatever, I'll be here. I grabbed your hotel room key for you," he huffs.

"Great," I groan. "I don't know how you do this, man. This amount of traveling . . . I already hate it."

"Nah, I love it. I mean, what else do I have back home? I love seeing different places and seeing different women." I can practically hear him wink through the phone.

"Dude, whatever. I was just calling to tell you I'm on my way," I grumble.

"Okay, listen, man. Sorry, but we will be back soon. It'll go by fast," Liam states.

"Yeah, thanks, see you soon." I hang up with Liam before he can say anything else. I'm not in the mood right now.

I drive a few more miles, thinking about the past few weeks, the rain in my Jeep, the movies, cuddles, showers, and everything else. Sarah is just on a constant loop in my mind.

I wonder what she's doing now . . . She's probably cuddled on her couch with Trixie.

I'm immediately jealous of that damn cat, while simultaneously missing her, too.

I look at the clock. It's late, but I think my mom should still be awake. I dial her on speaker phone to check in.

"Hi, sweetie!" My mom answers almost immediately after the first ring. "Good to hear from you! I miss you. How are you, hun?"

I can't even get a word in, and I immediately start to laugh. I miss her.

"I'm good, Mom. How are you? I've been worried about you!" Sorrow seeps into my voice. I immediately feel guilty that I haven't called her sooner.

"Oh hush. If you were that worried, you would've called your dear old mama sooner!" She laughs and then sighs. "Just messing with you, hun! I'm good. I joined a widow's group, and it's been very peaceful. You know I miss your dad more than I can bear, but it's been nice to have a supportive group of people in my corner. Judy, from the group, has become a really dear friend. She comes for dinner once a week. That's been nice. It's nice to have someone to talk to and understands. She's funny too, you'd like her."

"Of course, your younger brothers also barge in for dinner frequently, and I'm starting to feel like myself again. Just myself with a huge part of my heart missing, but I'm out of bed! I'm doing it. It takes a while to get up most mornings, but I'm getting the hang of it!"

I can almost hear her wistful smile through the phone. My heart twists at her words.

"Enough about me, though, sweet boy! How are you? How's business? Do you love it yet?" she asks.

"Uhhh, no, Mom," I laugh. "I'll never love it. This life isn't for me. I don't know how Dad did it. I just want to be home. Wherever home may be at this point."

"It was definitely no walk in the park for him, but he loved what he did, and he came home almost every weekend to see me. He also had a lot of large stretches where there wasn't much traveling at all. He didn't have that fancy deal with Starbucks, you know. Maybe you would like it more if it was less traveling like he did." She sighs. "Of course, you know, I just want you to be happy, and if you ain't happy with this job, that's fine. You'll find your calling, hun. Eric will take over so soon. You're in the home stretch! Unless you're calling to tell me you can't do it anymore?"

"Oh, not at all. I'm fine. I just . . . I was calling be-cause . . . I met someone." I let it slip without meaning to. I meant to tell her I just wanted to talk, just wanted to check on her, but the words came out.

"Oh my!" Mom shouts. "It's the call I've waited for my whole life! Tell me everything!" She is pure joy through the phone, and my heart squeezes at realizing how much I've missed hearing her happy.

I tell my mom everything, about how I first met Sarah, the blind date, and realizing I messed up. I tell her about her sister, Jess, the plan, and all the messages. When I went to The Poppy Pub and got stood up, only to drive back to my room that looks like the side of a teacup. I tell her about Sarah showing up and giving me a chance. I *don't* tell her about everything that happened that night, though. I tell her about the past week full of movies, conversation, and meals.

I explain her coffee shop in great detail, how amazing it is, and in turn, how amazing Sarah is. The coffee shop is a direct reflection of her and her talent.

When I finish, my mom says, "She sounds so special, sweetie. She sounds like a real keeper."

I smile at the phone in my lap as I pull up to a stoplight. "Yeah, she really is." I sigh.

CHAPTER FORTY-TWO

Sarah

I'm TIRED THE NEXT day from staying up with Jess, but I'm happy I did it. I'm going to miss that little shithead.

The interviews the next day go pretty crappy, but choices are slim in Daisy Ridge. I end up hiring a young girl, Emily, who just graduated from high school. She doesn't interview super well, but given her age, I think she just doesn't have much experience with interviewing. I decide to give her a chance. She can only work part-time while she is taking online college classes, but part-time is probably fine for now.

I'm not sure exactly how much help I'll need yet anyway. I'm so hesitant because it's only been Carol and me for a while, with Jess working part-time and helping us out.

I spend the next two weeks training Emily. We work through all the drink recipes, the cash register, the inventory, and customer service. She picks everything up super quickly, and I'm pretty happy with my choice of hire.

Emily is actually a natural and reminds me a lot of myself when I first started working at Carnation. Carol is grumpy about me hiring someone so young, and every time she comments on it, I can't help but roll my eyes at her.

I work hard prepping and preparing the new and improved Daisy Ridge Coffee Co. for the influx I hope we will see after Tracee shares about us.

We work on strategies for if the lines start to get longer, how we will staff more people, and where they would be stationed. I re-write my employee handbook and work on training Carol to be a manager on the off chance things really start to take off.

We might fail when this is all said and done, but I work hard anyway. I prepare for every single outcome. The prep helps me keep my mind off Ethan being away and the loneliness I feel at night now.

When the day Tracee's content gets published finally arrives, we *do* see a nice influx. So much so, that all four of us work past closing. Jess, Carol, Emily, and I work non-stop in the days following as well, and it only gets busier.

I've never been more tired when the day ends. I'm not even watching movies or reading at night anymore. I feed Trixie, shower, and get into bed.

I'm absolutely giddy when I put the now hiring sign back up a few days later. It turns out, I think I'll need a couple more people. When I put the sign up, Carol and I even hug and cry happy tears together. "I'm so proud of you, hun! You're doing the damn thing! Your mama is probably crying happy tears with us right now." She smiles wide at me as her eyes fill with more tears.

I cry too. I thought this business was going to go under when I heard the news of the incoming competition. Now I think this town just might be big enough for the both of us. While I'm still not thrilled about it, my following on our social media account is growing day by day. It feels like we've become the spot all the girls want to stop at on their way to the city.

So that night, when I sit down to finally get some rest, I do something I never thought I would.

I reach out to the phone number I took a picture of almost a month ago. I call about the vacant store that used to be Carnation Coffee. I don't even feel guilty anymore. That space deserves to be returned to its former glory. I feel confident now that I can be the one to do it.

> *Dear Chaiguy87,*
>
> *I miss you. It seems silly. How long have we even known each other?*
>
> *The cafe is doing so well, and honestly, it's thanks to you. Tracee's videos have been a hit and brought in an amazing amount of business so far.*
>
> *There is a video of Carol that has gone viral. Groups of girls keep coming in, asking to take pictures with her. Apparently, Carol is TikTok famous now, and you know Carol—she's eating it up. Wearing even wilder outfits lately. She even got herself a button that says "As Seen on TV." It's ridiculous, and she keeps saying she needs to make herself a "Tic Tac account."*

There is apparently another video of you gushing about the coffee shop that has gone viral. People keep asking what time the dreamy man usually comes in. I have to tell them that, sadly, you're away on business. There is usually a chorus of whines following that statement.

Things are going well, really well. I reached out to a couple of other influencers in the Southwest to keep the momentum going. We are scheduling more visits, and I'm excited about the future.

I secretly think this situation, while shitty, gave me the exact push I needed. These are things I should've done for my business a while ago. I just got comfortable with how my life was.

Anyway, hope everything is going well at the new job site! I can't wait to see you again soon!

TTFN XOX Coffeegal13

CHAPTER FORTY-THREE

Ethan

EVERYTHING IS PRETTY SHITTY without Sarah.

Mostly because I hate my job. Now that I spent a couple of weeks looking forward to Sarah at the end of my work day, my job sucks even more now. It's all just work.

There isn't much to look forward to except for emails and phone calls with Sarah and planning my future.

It's funny because a few short weeks ago, the future terrified me. I didn't know what I wanted or what I'd do next. The thought of it all gave me knots in my stomach and gray hairs on my head.

Now planning the future is what is keeping me sane. The idea of what comes next brings a smile to my face instead of anxiety to my stomach.

Sarah and I still send daily emails like before. Now we also text throughout the day, and sometimes, we even FaceTime or talk over the phone. One night, we talked on the phone until Sarah fell asleep. I plugged my phone in and put it on speaker. It was slightly weird of me, but I wasn't ready to hang up on her. When she woke up around 3 a.m., it woke me up, and we both laughed sleepily.

At this point, we basically communicate all day when we aren't working.

She's been working a lot, though. From what it sounds like, the coffee shop has really taken off in a big way, and I'm sad I don't get to witness that firsthand. I wish someone was there recording her success. She deserves every minute of it. I try to keep reminding myself, though, that soon I'll be there.

Today, I'm on-site. We start the construction process on this one today after weeks of arguing over development plans and fighting with city planning. I'm standing here currently listening to Liam flirt with one of the girls on our new job site, and I roll my eyes as I listen to them. I can't wait to get back to Daisy Ridge, so I shoot Sarah a text.

> **One more week, can't wait. Miss you! <3**

> **Just in time, I just thinking about how much I miss your tongue.. I mean you ;)**

I laugh at her reply. I'm eager to reveal my plans for the future. I'm also slightly nervous she won't be on board, but I think I know Sarah pretty well now. I think she will be excited about our future *together*.

Two days later, my brother, Eric, comes to town. He came to the new job site to check-in. He has a break from school right now, and I'm excited to spend some time with him. I haven't seen any members of my family in a while. I won't lie, as soon as I see him walking up, I start to feel emotional. He looks so much like my dad. He waves at me from a distance, and as soon as he is close enough, I pull him in.

I slap his back in a big bear hug. "How you doing, little bro?" I say as I release him.

He smiles at me. "We are all hanging in there. How are *you* doing?" He raises his eyebrows in question.

I laugh. "I'm actually pretty good. The business is not only surviving but thriving—so it's ready for you at any time." I pause, not sure what to say next. "And I met someone . . . She's . . . well, she's the one. So say the word, and I'm throwing this all happily to you. I'm ready to be done."

"You found . . . someone?" He looks at me, shocked. "Like . . . here?" He looks around at the job site and all the crew members surrounding us.

I laugh again. "Nah, she's in Daisy Ridge, near our last job site. She's . . . well, she's amazing. She owns a coffee shop there. She is such a talented woman. I can't wait for you to meet her. I especially can't wait for Mom to meet her; she's going to absolutely love her."

Eric smiles big at me. "I won't lie. It's weird to see you like this. I've never seen you this . . . happy. You're smiling and laughing. It's . . . weird." He chuckles. "But I'm so happy for you, man. And trust me, I'm more than ready to take over for you . . . Unfortunately, I've got a few more months of school, so just don't bail until then."

I glare at him. "Of course I won't bail on you. This business means a lot to you. It means a lot to Mom, and as much as I may hate the job, it means a lot to me. I wouldn't do that to Dad. He loved this. Sometimes I wish I shared some biology with him, any really. Maybe then I'd love this job and life would look a lot different for me." I pause, trying to fight the emotion clogging my throat. "I used to wish he was my biological dad every day, but now . . . well, I wouldn't have Sarah if that were the case. I wouldn't be me." I give Eric a sad smile.

Eric gives me one back. "You know Dad never cared about biology, man. You were his, the same way I am. It never mattered to him. He'd be proud of you, and not just because of his business, but because you found happiness in the process. That happiness is what he always wanted for you, for all of us."

"You'll find it too, Brother. I know you will. I'm just bummed Dad isn't here to see it all." I grab my brother's shoulder and start leading him toward our job site. I need to change the subject before we both start crying. "Let me show you around. You can see the future plans too. Help me decide what you're working on in three months."

"Sounds good, man," he says, "but I'm not finding anyone, not anytime soon. That's the complete last thing on my mind right now." He shrugs.

"Eh, I've been told that's when you find it . . . " I smile at him.

Dear Coffeegal13,

I'm so excited about all the stuff happening online. I knew if more people knew about your shop—business would start moving. There happen to be a lot of people who pass through your town.

I saw my brother today, and it was good. I've missed my family, and I don't think I realized how much I missed them until now. Seeing him did make me a little sad, though; I miss my dad a lot.

Eric looks great, though, and there is an end in sight now. I won't be stuck doing a job I hate forever. I've known that, but it's nice to have an actual date I'm working toward now.

I told Eric all about you, and he is excited to meet you someday.

& I miss you too. It's not weird, and we are going to keep saying it. It's us. Working this job sucks even worse without looking forward to seeing you at the end of the day.

Text me tonight,
XOX, Chaiguy87

A week later, we are heading out for Daisy Ridge. Unfortunately, I'm supposed to share a shitty hotel room at the Motel 6 with Liam this time, for financial purposes. We aren't staying at the Lavender Dreams this time around, sadly. I kind of miss that little floral tea cup room. It definitely looked and smelled like my grandmother's linen closet, but I have a lot of happy memories there now.

Luckily for me, though, I don't think I'll be spending a single second of my time in the new hotel room with Liam. My plan is to be with Sarah during the very few hours of free time I have, and my hope is she will want me to stay the night with her after I reveal my plans for the future.

It's just a quick weekend trip, and I already wish I had more time in Daisy Ridge. For now, though, this is all I get, and I'm going to make the most of it. I'm going to enjoy being in my happy place with Sarah.

We arrive at Daisy Ridge on a Friday morning. We spend all day in meetings with executives walking through the new location, marking imperfections with blue tape for the construction crew. Once our part is done, Starbucks will come in and add its decor and flair. Sarah still has about a full month until she needs to worry about her competition. I've been updating her as much as I'm allowed to.

By Friday afternoon, I am bouncing my foot up and down, impatiently waiting for the moment I can go to Sarah's. I want to see how her business is doing. She said in her daily emails that when Tracee's content went live, they saw a nice influx in business. She also said she has hired two new employees.

I can't wait to be back at Daisy Ridge Coffee Co. In the blink of an eye, it's become my favorite place in the world. It's a direct reflection of Sarah, and it's absolutely beautiful in every way.

I keep checking my watch, keep tapping my foot, just waiting for the meeting and our day to be over.

Around four p.m., they finally end the meetings, and I shake hands with everyone. I tell everyone I will see them tomorrow, and I tell Liam I may or may not see him later.

He winks at me and says, "Go get 'em, tiger."

I take off as fast as possible for the place—*and person*—I love.

Chapter Forty-Four

Sarah

I GET A BUZZ on my phone. It's a notification for another job application, and I smile.

I really never thought I would need this many employees. Carol, Emily, and my newest hire, Amanda, are all working right now. I let Carol help me pick Amanda, and of course, she is closer to Carol's age, which made her so happy. I have this odd, and slightly sad, feeling I may not be Carol's 'bestie for the restie' anymore.

I let them all know I'm heading to the back for a few minutes and to holler if they need me.

In unison, Carol and Amanda say, "Yes, Boss Lady!" and Emily starts laughing. I let Carol train Amanda, and it shows. I laugh too and give them a little salute.

We are all having so much fun working together. We've only been together about three weeks now, but it feels like we've known each other for years.

I smile as I walk back to my office, because I don't know how I got so lucky lately. Business is great. I'm placing supply orders twice as much as I used to. I sit down at my computer and take a second to just soak it all in.

I open up my computer, excited to pull up this new job application. When I see the name, though, my stomach does a pancake flip. It can't be right . . . I click out of it and open it again, but the name still reads *Ethan Stone*. I smile widely as I start to read the cover letter attached.

Just then, Carol hollers, "Boss Lady! You're going to want to head out here!" I quickly leap up, worried something has gone wrong. When I turn out into the lobby and face the register, though, my eyes fill with tears.

Ethan stands there looking disheveled in a suit. His hair is a gorgeous mess. It looks like he ran his hand through it a few too many times today. His tie is loosened, like he wanted it off but was in too much of a hurry to bother.

I run around the counter full speed toward him as he spreads his arms out. I reach out and wrap my arms around his neck as he embraces me tightly in a hug. I press my lips to his neck as I take in a deep breath of him. God, I've missed him. I pull my face back, and he looks at me and whispers, "Hi." I smile up at him.

I kiss him like no one is watching, because I don't care. Five weeks was too long, and I need to enjoy every second I have left with him. When I pull my face back, he chuckles and says, "I missed you too."

Carol shouts, "Get a room, Boss Lady!"

I glance over at her with a laugh. "Are you good to close up with our newbies?"

Carol sighs. "Yes, yes, go on—get outta here already!" She waves us toward the doors, and I laugh. I'm so grateful for Carol taking on more lately and so grateful I hired new girls. I feel so comfortable walking away to spend a couple of hours with Ethan right now.

Ethan looks at Carol, winks, and then lifts me up over his shoulder and says, "Great! Sounds like permission to me!" and takes off for the front door.

I squeal and swat at his muscular back. "Put me down, ya big oaf!" I say, giggling.

Once we make it out front, he puts me down and grabs my hand in his. We make our way around back and head up to my apartment. I can practically hear my heart pounding in my chest with excitement. I honestly wouldn't be surprised if Ethan could hear it too. It's pumping so hard.

We climb up the stairs, and once inside, Trixie comes barreling toward us and leaps up at Ethan as he catches her perfectly in his arms.

She immediately starts purring, and Ethan scratches behind her ear. "Aw, missed you too, sweet girl!" he purrs back at her. She meows at him aggressively, trying to capture all of his attention.

I laugh. "What about me? Do you two need a room?"

"Hey now, there is enough love for both of my favorite girls." He smiles at me, and I melt. My heart skips a beat at the casual use of the word *love*.

"Well, enough of that. I need to ask you a serious question." I cross my arms in front of my chest and put on my very best serious face.

"Oh, you do?" He plays coy.

"I do indeed . . . Why on earth did I just get a job application from you?" I swat at him playfully, and he puts Trixie down on the floor.

"Well because in about two more months, I'm going to need a job . . . and I'd really like it to be with you, at Daisy Ridge Coffee Co." He smiles down at me.

"And why on earth would you want to do that? You don't even live here?" I ask.

"Oh, but I will, because you see, a friend of mine is moving off to Rose Point—going to go after her dreams of being the best florist ever, as she is destined to be. She needs out of her lease in order to make her dreams happen, and it just so happens that Daisy Ridge is my new favorite place in the world. So she is signing her lease over to me in just two short months." He smiles at me and reaches for my hand. He squeezes it gently before reaching for my other hand.

We stand in my kitchen holding hands and smiling at each other like a couple of complete fools. He starts to talk softly. "Now the only problem is, in order to take over her lease, I need a job here, and I'm afraid after one shift a couple months ago in Daisy Ridge Coffee Co., nothing else will do. It's unfortunately my dream job now; I *must* work there. I'm hoping the fact that the owner just might be the love of my life . . . well, I'm hoping she will give me a chance." He smiles down at me. It's a nervous smile full of hope.

It's quite possibly my new favorite smile of his, this just-admitted-he-kinda-loves-me smile. "Well," I say, "I suppose, perhaps I could use another set of hands, and it may be kind of nice to bring a man into our mix." I grin at him. "Especially because in about six months, I'll need some employees for Carnation Coffee too." I'm afraid my skin may wrinkle forever from how wide I'm smiling.

He smiles too. "Did you really do it?" he whispers, like it's a secret meant just for us.

"I did. This pesky man I absolutely hated told me to, and I was hesitant at first, but . . . the time felt right, especially after Daisy Ridge Coffee Co.'s *big boom* on the travel sites. As it turns out, the people of Carnation Springs are dying for some Daisy Ridge Coffee too." I grip his hands and wait with bated breath to hear what he thinks.

His one eye waters, but no tear falls. He whispers, "I'm really fucking proud of you, Sarah. It hasn't been long, and I want to take things slow, but I want you to know: The only future I see is with you. I know we've only known each other for a few months, but my soul has known yours for a lifetime. I can't imagine a life without you, and I want to support you. I want you to achieve your dreams, and I want to be there to help in every way I can."

I smile widely at him.

"I want to be with you too, Ethan." I kiss him.

He pauses for a second. "What about the pesky man? Do you still hate him?" Ethan whispers against my lips.

"Nope. Not even close. Not even a little bit. Not even at all." I smile against his lips, happy with my perfect use of an amazing movie quote.

He kisses me again.

EPILOGUE

Sarah

ONE YEAR LATER.

Carnation Coffee has been doing amazing. It's been open for about six months now, and it's a huge hit among travelers.

We recently hosted part of the Carnation Springs Singles' Night. This year, they had *four* locations for speed dating, and we were one of them. It was the most fun we've ever had while working, and it was amazing for business.

All the girl groups that were in town for Singles' Night came for coffee all weekend long.

It was a fun weekend to be in the coffee business. Tracee even came by with some of her influencer friends to cover the whole Singles' Night event. They made a new post with a girls' trip weekend itinerary in Carnation Springs.

She was so excited to see that Ethan and I are now officially together. She says that someday, she wants to write a blog post on our love story.

Ethan's brother, Eric, finally took over BloomStone Builders about nine months ago now, and it's doing great! They are still working with Starbucks, but now he also has a contract with In-N-Out Burger. I've put in my official request for them to build one over in our neck of the woods, but only time will tell.

Ethan and I are doing amazing. My two little coffee shops are thriving right now, and while that may not last forever in today's economy, I'm enjoying the present, and so is he.

I hustle around with moving boxes. Unpacking sucks, and carrying boxes and furniture up a flight of stairs stinks. It's been a long time since I've moved, so I kind of forgot how brutal it is. Thank goodness the weather is beautiful right now, because I think if we moved in the heat of summer, I would totally cry.

Luckily, I didn't have to do a whole lot of packing. We moved Ethan's things to our new little place in Carnation Springs. It's right above Carnation Coffee, just like our place in Daisy Ridge, and we split our time between the two locations. I don't think that's permanent. We've already talked about eventually letting Carol or another manager rent out the space. I'm being practical and keeping all of Ethan's things until we get married.

Ethan already offered to get rid of his belongings and talks about forever. I'm following the advice from Carol and enjoying every second of it right now. I definitely can't imagine my life without Ethan, though; he's everything.

I've grown a lot over the past year and realized with my mom dying at such a young age, I just want to enjoy every bit of life and love this world gives me.

Jess moved to Rose Point about ten months ago, and while it started out *incredibly* rocky for her, her life ended up exactly as it should have. I'm excited for both of our futures and continuing our weekly dinners with Dad.

Carol and Smithy are officially a 'thing.' They kiss in front of the whole damn town, although no one really knows if they are officially 'official.'

The new employees have been amazing, Ethan included. Ethan is still just an employee and says he wants to stay that way forever. He says these shops are my babies, and he's happy to just make the coffee and be the owner's 'soon-to-be husband.' I roll my eyes every time he says it.

I'm totally lost in my thoughts while unpacking. I don't even hear Ethan sneaking up behind me before he grabs me around the waist. He picks me up and twirls me around our new second living room. I laugh, and he sets me down on top of the couch.

"You ready to break in the new place?" He winks at me.

"We don't even have the bed set up yet, ya big goof!" I playfully smack at his chest.

"I don't know, this couch . . . looks fine to me," he says with a smirk before smacking my ass.

I laugh and jump up onto him, wrapping both legs around his waist.

I kiss him hard, grabbing his face in both my hands before whispering to him, "I fucking love you."

He lifts me up and then gently sets me down on the couch, pressing his body into mine. "I fucking love you, too," he says before kissing me again.

A year ago, Ethan thought he needed to be more, find some bigger purpose and career path, but it turns out, we are both perfectly fine being *just* Coffee People.

Coffee People
DRINKS

SARAH'S SPECIAL

- Two shots of espresso
- ¼ oz of Chocolate Syrup
- ¼ oz of Coconut Syrup
- ¼ oz of Caramel Syrup
- 8 oz of your preferred milk
- (optional Caramel Drizzle)

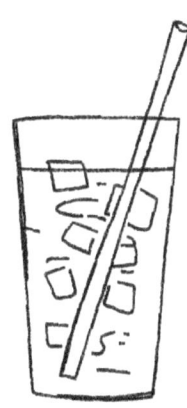

ETHAN'S DIRTY CHAI

- Your favorite chai tea bags, I use Trader Joe's Chai or Tazo, which can be found in most grocery stores (2 bags, steeped in 3/4 cup water)
- Brown sugar syrup or other sweetener of choice (1/4 cup)
- Strong coffee (1/2 cup)
- Oat milk (3/4 cup)

Coffee People
DRINKS

JESS' ICED TEA

- 16 ounces of your favorite black tea, iced or hot.
- 1 ounce of honey syrup or honey
- Splash of Half and Half Cream

CAROL'S SMOOTHIE

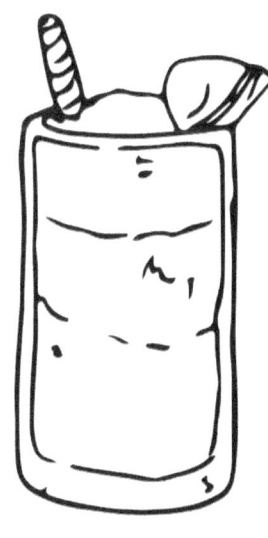

- ¾ Cup of Brewed Coffee, cooled in the fridge
- One Frozen Ripe Banana
- One Teaspoon of Vanilla
- One Teaspoon of Chocolate Sauce
- ¼ Cup of Coconut Milk
- Ice -Blend all ingredients in blender

Sneak Peek
FLOWER PEOPLE

Ashley Claire

CHAPTER ONE

Jess

I FUCKED UP.

I showed up for my first day of work at my dream job. I was looking like a million bucks, and feeling like a trillion—and the owner was *him*.

The guy who shoved me out of his home the morning before, telling me he wasn't looking for anything serious.

I didn't care at that moment yesterday morning. I figured I'd never see the asshole again, but now he is my *boss*. He's seen me naked. He's done absolutely magical things with my body. I've had more orgasms with the man standing in front of me than my most recent ex-boyfriend of four months.

The night we spent together felt like something. I'm so naive. I'm probably too young for him, or just too stupid. I have to be an idiot to think we had some kind of magical connection. I was a giddy little school girl, and he said I needed to leave.

I can barely look him in the eyes, and yet, I have to work for him.

48 hours earlier...

I've finally fucking made it.

I honestly thought I'd die alone in the small town of Daisy Ridge, but I somehow got my dream job. I'm going to be a lead florist at the cutest flower shop in Rose Point. Blossom Bliss Boutique is the most gorgeous flower shop I've ever seen. It's a little maroon store front, tightly wedged in between the city buildings. The name is written in script across the top of the building; buckets and buckets of flowers cascade down the storefront. Their captivating colors draw you in. Inside there is every style of floral arrangement you could ever imagine.

I did several interviews with them over the phone. Eventually, I went in and did a few arrangements for the current lead florist, Becky, who absolutely loved me! I mean, how could she not?

Unfortunately, the owner's daughter was home sick the day I came in to do my arrangements. He let Becky make the call. She said it was a no-brainer: I had to be the new florist. I felt slightly weird about taking a job in such a small place without meeting the owner, but I'm sure he is awesome. With a flower shop like that, how could he not be?

I moved into my new apartment on Stem Street, and my best friend, Lindsey, and I are going out to celebrate tonight. Lindsey owns the cutest bookstore in Rose Point. Someday, I hope I can own my own flower shop, but for now I'm just happy to be here in the city.

Don't get me wrong, I miss Daisy Ridge. I miss my big sister and dad like crazy, but I have a lot of fun friends in the city. I'll likely still see my sister and dad once a week for dinner, so I don't feel too bad. I was just destined for city life; the small-town vibes never really fit me.

So tonight, I'm ready to party it up with my bestie! We are going to Bloomsy Bar for our first few drinks, and then going over to Stem Street Station, that way I'm nice and close to home. I'm planning on getting crazy tonight. I haven't spent a night in the city in a *long* time, and Lindsey and I are going to have the freaking best time now that I *live* here. I seriously can't wait to spend every day with her.

It still feels surreal.

I'm still unpacking my new apartment; there are boxes all over my tiny new studio. It's so small compared to the two bedroom I was renting in Daisy Ridge. I'm probably going to have to downsize because right now the boxes are stacked in every direction higher than my head. It's a problem for a later Jess though, because right now, I'm focused on going out.

There is a knock at the door, and I swing it open, screeching loudly as I do. "AHHHHHH!" Lindsey shouts while jumping up and down on the other side.

"You're here! You have a place! We doin' the damn thing! We are making dreams come true, bitch!" she shouts excitedly.

My next-door neighbor, Phyllis, who I had the *joy* of meeting earlier, swings open her door. Lindsey turns to look at her. Phyllis sticks her head out, glares at Lindsey and I, and then yells "Will you broads keep it down? I can't hear my damn television. I need to hear my Sixty Minutes!" and then slams her door shut again.

Lindsey turns back around to face me, whispering, "Oops, sorry," as her face twists into a grimace.

She and I start laughing quietly as I usher her into my studio and close the door behind her.

"Sweet neighbor you got there!" She moves her thumb back over her shoulder gesturing to where Phyllis lives. She looks around my new place, hands on her hips, before muttering, "I mean this in the nicest way, but this place is kind of a pit. Do you want me to help you unpack tonight instead of going out?"

"Hell no!" I shout at her. "It's my first night living in the same city as my best friend! We are going out to party and celebrate!"

"Okay, okay, I just know you start your new job in a couple days, it might be nice to not be cramped with boxes by then . . . " She gestures around to the array of boxes stacked high everywhere.

"Ugh, it's fine, Linds. I'll unpack tomorrow. Let's goooooo!" I pump my fist in the air, and she laughs.

"All right, let's get ready!" She turns toward my bathroom, carefully moving around all the boxes. It's an utter maze to get there, but we make it into my cramped bathroom, and she starts laughing.

"What's so funny?" I glare at her.

"Oh, nothing, it's just that this bathroom is not big enough for both of us to do makeup in." She laughs. "Got another mirror somewhere? I can just sit on some boxes, make a little vanity out of them?"

"You're being a bitch . . . " I mumble pulling a mirror out from a drawer. It's luckily the only bathroom drawer I already unpacked. I'm grateful I did, otherwise Lindsey would probably make another comment about how we shouldn't go out tonight.

"Do you have a speaker unpacked yet? I can put on some music?" She pulls her phone out of her jeans pocket.

"Yeah, it's on the counter," I say gesturing to where my tiny counter is. The counter isn't even big enough for two barstools, but I squeezed two in there anyway.

Lindsey starts playing her 'going out' playlist, which takes off with "Cruel Summer" by Taylor Swift, because we are Eras Tour girlies.

I plug in the curling iron so I can start curling my long, dark brown hair. I think my hair is my best feature. It holds curls so well, and I love to style it like old-school Hollywood. I typically use Sabrina Carpenter pictures as my inspiration. Her hair is so damn gorgeous.

While the curling iron heats up, I start cleaning off the makeup I'm currently wearing, so I can do a fresh style for tonight. You'll never see me without makeup on. I would be embarrassed as hell if someone saw me without makeup. My fair skin and bright blue eyes just don't have the same impact without makeup and my self-tanner.

Once I have my hair and makeup done, I rummage through a box with my heels in it. I'm the shortest of my friends and family, so I usually always wear heels. I'm only 5', so I wear heels to make my legs appear longer.

I find the sparkly black heels I was looking for, and make my way back through the maze of boxes to set them on the counter.

I look over at Lindsey, who did in fact create a little vanity out of boxes. She looks adorable. Lindsey doesn't do as much with her hair and makeup as I do, but she doesn't need it. She is naturally gorgeous. Her long, red hair cascades down in perfect beach waves. Her cheeks are lightly freckled highlighting her little blue eyes. She's wearing a gorgeous red crochet crop top that has a maroon bralette underneath. Her high-waisted jean shorts hug her curves perfectly.

She looks over at me while applying her lip gloss. "What are you going to wear tonight?"

I look down at the robe I'm currently wearing. "I don't know. I don't have everything unpacked yet . . . I'll definitely wear my signature black leather jacket."

"Well, duh!" She laughs. "You practically can't go anywhere without it."

I walk over to an open box of clothes on the floor and start rummaging through it. "Is a dress too much? What are the vibes we are going for tonight?" I say into the box.

"I mean . . . I'm wearing this." I turn, and Lindsey gestures to her current outfit.

"Ugh, okay, I mean, I'll probably wear a dress anyway," I grunt. I don't really feel confident in anything else lately.

"You do you, boo!" Lindsey smiles.

I pull out one of my favorite red dresses, a tight fitted red dress with halter straps that criss-cross at the neck.

Once I'm dressed, I fluff up my hair, running my fingers through it one last time. I touch up my makeup and apply my lip gloss.

I head out of the bathroom where Lindsey is waiting for me while texting on her phone.

"You ready to get crazy?" I ask her.

"Oh, I was born ready!" she says, and we laugh as we link our arms together and make our way out.

I'm planning on finding the hottest guy in this city tonight and making him mine.

Acknowledgements

I wrote a damn book. I never dreamed I'd say those words, and yet, here we are.

First and foremost, I would like to thank my husband. You're my best friend in the whole world, and the best decision I've ever made. Your endless support and love over the many years we've been together is all I ever need in life. If tomorrow the world absolutely hates this book, and I go up in flames—you're the only thing I need to survive. Thank you for dealing with my indecisiveness, and sticking with me while I figured out what the fuck I was doing with my life (much like Ethan in this book). But, hey we made it! I love you more than all the stars in the sky, and all the fish in the sea. You're literally everything. *XOXO*

To my kiddos, my little Peanut and Pickle—please always know your mom loves you an _insane_ amount. Every day I drop you off at school I'm sad, I wish I could still spend every second with you but I'm so proud of you both and the people you are becoming. You can both do absolutely *anything* you put your mind to! Whether you are a coffee barista or a neuro surgeon—I will be so happy to step aside and watch you shine! You will both do amazing things in this world!! P.S Please forgive me for always being the ultimate helicopter mom, I just love you both so much!

For the readers, thank you. Truly, from the bottom of my heart. You'll never know my gratitude for you taking the time to read this book. It means the world to me. I hope this is the worst book I ever write for you. I hope they only get better from here.

To my parents, Thank you for encouraging me to read and write throughout life. Thank you for always telling me I could be anything I wanted. Thanks for supporting me and being there for me when I needed you. Thanks for telling me to get back up and try again. Thanks for telling me to prove people wrong. I know some people aren't lucky enough to have supportive parents like you, and I truly hit the jackpot with both of you. I love you both so much. P.S. I'm sorry I'm now a romance writer who writes smut—please don't ever actually read this book. <3

Jenessa, my author bestie, neighbor, and life twin—I really couldn't have done this without you. I truly want to be you when I grow up because you are incredible in every damn way. While I should've done a lot of things sooner, like asking about publishing timelines, cover reveals, and how to *actually* publish a book—I did one thing right by forcing you to be my friend. I cannot wait until you make it big and we celebrate your massive success, because it's coming *so soon* friend!

Cassidy, Alexis, and Chelsey—thank you for ALPHA reading the hell out of this book. I know none of you had the time or energy—but you did it anyway, and I'll forever be grateful. Your edits and commentary made me keep going when I second-guessed all my life choices. I don't think I would've made this book without you.

Book Besties, you're the ultimate ride-or-die book club and I still don't know how I got so lucky. Silly me, I thought I'd start an awkward little book club with friends from all over my life. The only shared trait between us all is a love for books. I thought it would be so awkward, and I thought I would be stressed out about everyone getting along. It turns out, I didn't need to worry at all. You took a little idea for a book club and truly made a cult. A cult full of women, who do what they want with no remorse. A ride-or-die crew that does everything from sharing embarrassing sex stories, to letting someone vent, all the way to holding someone's hair back while they do a shot by my kitchen sink. I don't know where I'd be without you guys, but I know it wouldn't be half as fun. I love you all and your endless support.

Special shout-out to Chelsey and Tori, who showed up with soda and candy while I was editing. I honestly was spiraling out of control, and you have no idea how much I just needed someone to sit with me and be supportive. I think I really would've called it all off and gone into hiding that day if it wasn't for you.

Ironically, I'd like to thank Starbucks, who fueled most of the writing of this book. Although I'm sincerely upset about the discontinuation of the Spinach Feta Wrap, and even more upset about the lack of the return of coconut syrup in the past few years. Thanks for fueling this book on your Sugar Cookie Latte.

Shout-out to all the Independent and locally owned coffee shops I frequented during the writing of this book—you're superior in every way.

Thank you to coffee in general. My obsession with you is unparalleled, and therefore the first book I ever wrote clearly had to involve *you*.

Emily, meeting you at Readers of the Valley changed my life, and messaging with you on social media has pushed me through when I wanted to quit. As writers, I think we share a lot of the same traits and anxieties. Thanks for being a support system I didn't know I needed. A support system you probably didn't know you were.

Thank you to EJL Editing, @ejlediting, for taking on a brand new author with no experience and editing this book. Your work is greatly appreciated!

Thank you to Athira, at @gloinkdesigns for working on ALL the art for this book. You made every character exactly the way I imagined them. I cannot thank you enough for your countless hours making these characters come to life.

Allie, @baddecisionsbookclub, thank you for hyping me up, reading, and editing. You're a gem of a human, and I'm so lucky to know you!

Finally, thank you <u>again</u> to Cassidy and Chelsey for their final proofread. You really know how to hype a girl up and put her at ease! The fact that you read this book more than once means the world.

ABOUT THE AUTHOR

Ashley Claire

Ashley Claire is a cliché millennial Disney adult and hard-core Swiftie. Residing in hell.. Oops, I mean sunny Arizona. She is the mother of two amazing kids and married to her best friend. She has always been an avid reader with a passion for books. Ashley started her journey teaching high school and eventually moved on to be an editor and content writer for many years before deciding to drop everything and risk it all by writing her own stories and novels.

Ashley enjoys coffee, nerds gummy clusters, and pickles. She loves planning and hosting book clubs, and hopes everyone finds a group of bookish friends to share life with. The more book clubs we have in the world—- the merrier!

Follow along for updates on what Ashley has planned
next!
Instagram: @ashleyclairebooks
Facebook: ashleyclairebooks
Website: www.ashleyclairebooks.com

www.ingramcontent.com/pod-product-compliance
Lightning Source LLC
Chambersburg PA
CBHW050014120726
47903CB00006B/1761